AR
RL 3.8
Pts.4
MG

DATE DUE			

Logan Likes Mary Anne!

Ann M. Martin

GREY CASTLE PRESS

This book is for my old baby-sitters,
Maura and Peggy

First Grey Castle Edition, Lakeville, Connecticut, September, 1988

Published in large print by arrangement with Scholastic, Inc., New York.

Printed in the U.S.A.

The Library of Congress Cataloging in Publication Data Available.

ISBN 0-0942545-71-0   (lg. print)
ISBN 0-0942545-81-8   (lib. bdg.: lg. print)

CHAPTER 1

It was the last day of summer vacation. I couldn't believe more than two months had sped by since the end of seventh grade. One day the weather had been fresh and cool with the promise of summer and fun, and now it was stale and hot with the promise of autumn and school. Tomorrow my friends and I would become eighth-graders. An awful lot had happened over the summer. In fact, it had been a more eventful summer than usual. Something important had happened to every single member of the Baby-sitters Club.

I guess that, first of all, I should tell you what the Baby-sitters Club is, in case you don't know. The club consists of me (I'm Mary Anne Spier) and my friends Kristy Thomas, Dawn Schafer, Claudia Kishi, and Stacey McGill. The five of us run a business, which Kristy started. We baby-sit for the kids in our neighborhoods, and we have a lot of fun — and earn pretty much money, too. We meet three times a week to take calls from people who need baby-sitters, and also sometimes to gossip and fool around. But we're very professional about the way we run our business.

Anyway, here's what happened to us over the summer. I'll start with Kristy, since she's the president of the club, and since her event was the biggest and most exciting of all. Her mother got married again and Kristy was her bridesmaid! Honest. She wore a long dress and her first pair of shoes with heels. Claudia and Dawn and Stacey and I were guests at the wedding. And *then* Kristy and her family (her two older brothers Sam and Charlie, and her little brother David Michael) moved out of their old house, which was next door to mine, and across town to her stepfather's mansion. Kristy's really got a good deal in her new place — she has anything she wants (within reason) plus built-in baby-sitting charges. Andrew and Karen, her little stepbrother and stepsister, spend every other weekend (and some in-between time, too) at Watson's. Watson is Kristy's stepfather.

Then there's Claudia Kishi. Claudia is the vice-president of our club. We always hold our meetings in her room, since she has her own phone and even her own private phone number. Claudia's summer event was the saddest of all, but it has a happy ending. Her grandmother Mimi (who lives with the Kishis, and who's a favorite of the Baby-sitters Club) had a stroke one night in July. She had to stay in the hospital for a long time and she still has to have physical therapy, but she's getting better. She can walk and talk, and someday (maybe) she'll be able to use her right hand a little more.

Dawn Schafer is my new best friend. She's the official alternate officer of the club, which means she can take over the duties of anyone who has to miss a meeting. Her family used to live in California, but her parents got divorced, so her mother moved Dawn and her younger brother Jeff all the way across country to Stoneybrook, Connecticut. Claudia and Kristy and I grew up here, but New England has been kind of an adjustment for Dawn. Anyway, over the summer, Dawn and Jeff got to fly to California to visit their father, and (after they'd come back) Dawn discovered a secret passage in the old farmhouse she lives in!

The fourth member of the club is Stacey McGill. She's our treasurer, and also sort of a newcomer to Stoneybrook. She moved here exactly one year ago from big, glamorous, exciting New York City. Stacey, by the way, is sort of glamorous and exciting herself. That's why she and Claudia are best friends. They're both sophisticated and love wearing flashy clothes and weird jewelry and doing things to their hair. The two of them really stand out in a crowd, and I've always been envious of them.

Anyway, Stacey's summer excitement was mine, too. We got jobs as mother's helpers with one of the families we sit for and went with them to the beach — Sea City, New Jersey. We stayed in Sea City for two weeks and not only had a great time, but found boys we liked! I guess that wasn't such a big deal for Stacey, but it was a big deal for me. I'm kind of shy and tend to be on the quiet side. I'd never been very interested in boys, either. This wasn't because I didn't like them; it was because I was afraid of them. I used to think, What do you say to a boy? Then I realized you can talk to a boy the same way you talk to a girl. You just have to choose your topics more carefully. Obviously, with a boy, you can't talk about bras or cute guys you see on TV, but you can talk about school and movies and animals and sports (if you know anything about sports).

When Stacey and I were in Sea City, Stacey started out by being a real pain. She fell in luv (as she always writes it) with this gorgeous lifeguard who was years too old for her, and left me on my own. With no one my age around, I started talking to this nice-looking boy who was hanging around on the beach because he was a mother's helper, too. We really hit it off. We talked about lots of things, and by the time I had to leave Sea City, we had exchanged rings with our initials on them. We bought them on the boardwalk. I don't know if we'll really write to each other (as we promised), but it's nice to know boys aren't aliens from the planet Snorzak or something.

Ding-dong. The doorbell. I wasn't sure how long I'd been lying on my bed daydreaming. I looked at my watch. It was almost time for our last Baby-sitters Club meeting of the summer.

"Coming!" I called.

I ran out of my bedroom, down the stairs, and through the hall to the front door. I peeped through the window. Dawn was standing on the steps. She sometimes comes to my house before a meeting, and then we walk over to Claudia's together.

"Hi!" she greeted me. Dawn was fussing with her hair. She has the longest hair of anyone I know. It's even longer than Claudia's. And it's pale, pale blonde. Dawn was wearing a pretty snappy outfit — hot-pink shorts with a big, breezy island-print shirt over a white tank top.

"Hi," I replied. "You look really terrific. Is that shirt new?"

Dawn nodded. "Dad sent it to me from California."

"Ooh, don't tell Kristy," I said.

"I know. I won't."

Kristy never hears from her real father. He hasn't been very nice to her, or to her brothers. He doesn't even send them birthday cards anymore. I'm glad she's got Watson now. If she'll just let herself like him a little more . . .

"We better go," said Dawn.

"Okay, I'm ready. Let me make sure I have my house key." I found my key and locked the front door. I'm usually the only one home during the day. My dad is a lawyer and he works long hours, I don't have any brothers or sisters, and my mother died when I was little. I barely remember her. Sometimes it's lonely at my house. I wish I had a cat.

Dawn and I crossed my front yard, and I stopped to check our mailbox.

"Aughh!" I shrieked when I opened the box. "It's here! It came!"

"What did?" asked Dawn, looking over my shoulder.

6

"*Sixteen* magazine. Oh, no! I'm dying! Look who's on the cover. It's Cam Geary! Isn't he adorable? The last issue had an article about him, but here's his gorgeous picture — " (I gasped) " — and a poster of him, too. A free poster!"

Dawn looked at me, amazed. "You sure have changed this summer, Mary Anne," she said. "I've hardly ever heard you talk so much. And I've *never* seen you go this crazy over a boy."

I flinched, remembering how, not long ago, I'd been accusing Stacey of talking about boys too much. But Dawn didn't seem annoyed.

We crossed the street and Claudia's lawn. Dawn rang the Kishis' bell.

"But Cam is a*dorable*," I said, hugging the magazine to me. "It's those eyes of his. They're so . . . so . . ."

"Hello, girls," Mimi greeted us, speaking slowly and clearly. The Kishis are Japanese and Mimi has always spoken English with an accent, but she isn't hard to understand. She speaks slowly now because of the stroke. "The other girls are here. They are in Claudia's room," she told us.

"We're the last ones?" I cried. "We better hurry. Come on, Dawn." I paused long enough to give Mimi a kiss. Then Dawn and I raced upstairs. As we ran by Janine's room (Janine is Claudia's older sister), we called hello to her, but we didn't stop. We didn't stop until we were in Baby-sitters Club headquarters. We closed the door behind us and flopped on the floor. The good spots were already taken — Stacey and Claudia were lying on the bed, and Kristy was sitting in the director's chair as usual. (She loves being in charge.)

"How did you get over here so early?" Dawn asked Kristy. Now that Kristy lives across town, she depends on her big brother Charlie to drive her to and from meetings. The Baby-sitters Club pays him to do that. It's part of running our business.

Kristy shrugged. "Charlie wanted to leave early. He was on his way to the shopping center. . . . Well, let's get started."

"Oh, Kristy," said Claudia. "We don't have to be in a rush. This is our last meeting of the summer. Nobody has to go anywhere. Let's have some refreshments first."

I grinned. Refreshments to Claudia are junk food. She's addicted to the stuff and has it hidden all over her room. I watched her reach inside her pillowcase. Then her hand emerged with two bags — one of gumdrops, one of pretzels. The pretzels were for everybody. The gumdrops were for herself and Kristy and me.

Dawn won't eat them because she says they're too unhealthy, and Stacey can't eat them because she has diabetes and has to stay on a strict diet — no extra sweets.

While Claudia passed around the food, Kristy got out our club record book and our notebook. She handed the record book to me. As secretary, it's my job to keep it up-to-date. I write down our baby-sitting appointments on the calendar pages and keep track of all sorts of things, such as our clients' addresses and phone numbers. Stacey, the treasurer, is in charge of recording the money we earn.

Our other book, the notebook, is a diary in which we write up every job we go on. Each of us is responsible for reading the book once a week or so. It takes a lot of time, but it's helpful to know what's happened at the houses where our friends have baby-sat.

"Any club business?" Kristy asked.

The rest of us shook our heads.

"Have you all read the notebook?"

"Yup," we replied.

"Okay. Great. Well, we'll just wait for the phone to ring."

The club meets three times a week — Monday, Wednesday, and Friday — from five-thirty until six. Our clients know that they can call

Claudia's number at those times and reach the five of us. They like the arrangement because they're bound to find a sitter.

I leaned back against Claudia's bed, opened *Sixteen*, and gazed at the free poster.

"Who's that? Cam Geary?" asked Stacey, peering over the edge of the bed at the picture.

I nodded. "Mr. Gorgeous."

"You know who he goes out with?" said Claudia.

"Who?" replied Stacey.

"Corrie Lalique."

"Corrie Lalique?" she shrieked. "The girl from 'Once Upon a Dream'? Does he really?"

"I read it in *Young Teen*," said Claudia.

"I read it in *Sixteen*," I added.

"But she's too old for him," Stacey protested.

"No she's not," Kristy spoke up. "She's fourteen."

Now it was my turn to be surprised. "You're kidding! Have you noticed the size of her — the size of her . . ."

"Chest?" supplied Claudia. "Well, she is kind of big, but believe me, Kristy's right. She's only fourteen. And she *is* going out with Cam."

"Boy — " I began, but I was interrupted by the phone.

Dawn answered it. "Hello, Baby-sitters

10

Club," she said. "Oh, hi! . . . When? . . . Okay. . . . Okay. I'll call you right back. . . . 'Bye."

Dawn hung up the phone. I was already holding the record book in my lap, opened to the appointment calendar.

"Mrs. Prezzioso needs someone for Jenny on Saturday afternoon, from four until about six-thirty," said Dawn.

This was met by groans. "I'll just check my own schedule," I replied. I'm the only one who likes Jenny at all. The others think she's bratty. It's a club rule that a job has to be offered to all the club members (not snapped up by the person who takes the call or something), but I didn't even bother to see if Kristy or Stacey or Claudia or Dawn was free. They wouldn't want the job. "Tell Mrs. Prezzioso I can sit," I said to Dawn as I noted my job in the appointment book.

Dawn called Mrs. Prezzioso back. When she got off the phone, Kristy's mother called needing a sitter for David Michael one afternoon when Kristy had a dentist's appointment. Then Dr. Johanssen called needing a sitter for Charlotte, and Mrs. Barrett called needing a sitter for Buddy, Suzi, and Marnie. It was a busy meeting. With school starting again, business was probably going to pick up a little. Everyone's schedules seemed to become more crowded.

The meeting was supposed to be over at six, but we all kind of hung around. No one wanted to end our last summer meeting. Finally I had to leave, though. So did Kristy. "See you in . . ." (gulp) ". . . school tomorrow!" she called, and I wanted to cry. Summer was really and truly over.

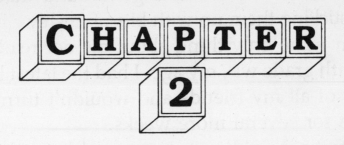

CHAPTER 2

Claudia and Stacey and I walked to school together the next morning, since the three of us live in the same neighborhood. It was the first time ever that Kristy and I hadn't walked off together on day number one of a school year. But Kristy had to take the bus from her new home. (Dawn, who lived not too far away, often took a different route to school, and sometimes her mother drove her there on her way to work.)

I was all set for eighth grade. My brand-new binder was filled with fresh paper; I had inserted neatly labeled dividers, one for each subject, among the paper; and a pencil case containing pens, pencils, an eraser, a ruler, and a pack of gum was clipped to the inside front cover. My lunch money was in my purse, the photo of Cam Geary was folded and ready to be displayed in my locker. (That was what the gum was for. You're not allowed to tape

13

things up in the lockers of Stoneybrook Middle School, so a lot of kids get around that rule by sticking them up with bits of freshly chewed gum.) The only thing about me not ready for eighth grade was my age. I had the latest birthday of all my friends and wouldn't turn thirteen for several more weeks.

Starting eighth grade seemed like a breeze to me. I'd been a chicken when we'd begun sixth grade, and I was going to be one of the youngest kids in the school. I hadn't been much better when we'd started seventh grade the year before. But now I felt like king of the hill. The eighth-graders were the oldest kids in school. We would get to do special things during the year. We would have a real graduation ceremony in June. After that, we would go on to the high school. Pretty important stuff.

But I couldn't decide whether to be excited or disappointed about the beginning of school. When we reached Stoneybrook Middle School, Stacey and Claudia and I just looked at each other.

Finally Claudia said, "Well, good-bye, summer."

Then Stacey started speaking in her Porky Pig voice. "Th-th-th-th-th-th-th-that's all, folks!" she exclaimed, waving her hand.

Claudia and I laughed. Then we split up.

There were three eighth-grade homerooms, and we were each in a different one. I went to my locker first, working half a piece of gum around in my mouth on the way. "Hello, old locker," I said to myself as I spun the dial on number 132. I opened the door. This was the only morning all year that my locker would be absolutely empty when I opened it. I pulled the poster of Cam Geary out of my notebook and set the notebook and my purse on the shelf of the locker. Then I unfolded the poster. I took the gum out of my mouth, checked the hall for teachers, and divided the gum into four bits, one for each corner. There. The poster stayed up nicely. I could look at Cam's gorgeous face all year.

I picked up my notebook and purse, closed my locker, and made my way upstairs. The hallways were already pretty crowded. Kids showed up early (or at least on time) for the first day of school.

My homeroom was 216, about as far from my locker as you could get. I entered it breathlessly, then slowed down. Suddenly I felt shy. Dawn was supposed to be in my homeroom, but she wasn't there yet. The room was full of kids I didn't know very well. And where was I supposed to sit? The teacher, Mr. Blake, was at his desk, but he looked busy. Had he planned on assigned seating? Could we sit wherever we wanted? I stood awkwardly by the door.

"Mary Anne! Hi!" said someone behind me.

Oh, thank goodness. It was Dawn.

I spun around. "Hi! I just got here," I told her.

Mr. Blake still wasn't paying attention to the kids gathering in his room.

"Let's sit in back," suggested Dawn.

So we did. We watched Erica Blumberg and Shawna Riverson compare tans. We watched a new kid creep into the room and choose a seat in a corner without looking at anyone. We watched three boys whisper about Erica and Shawna.

At last the teacher stood up. "Roll call," he announced, and the first day of school was truly underway.

This was my morning schedule:

> First period – English
> Second period – math
> Third period – gym (yuck)
> Fourth period – social studies
> Fifth period – lunch

My afternoon schedule wasn't so bad: science, study hall, and French class. But I thought my morning schedule was sort of heavy, and by lunchtime I was starved.

Kristy (who was in my social studies class) raced down to the cafeteria with me. We claimed the table we used to sit at last year with Dawn and some of our other friends. (Stacey and Claudia usually sat with their own group of kids.) In a moment Dawn showed up. She settled down and opened her bag lunch while Kristy and I went through the lunch line. Last year we'd brought our lunches, too. This year we'd decided brown bags looked babyish.

When we returned to the table with our trays, we were surprised to find Stacey and Claudia there with *their* trays. Since when had they decided to eat with us? We were good friends, but last year they always thought they were so much more sophisticated than we were. They liked to talk about boys and movie stars and who was going out with whom. . . . Had Stacey and Claudia changed, or had Kristy and Dawn and I? I almost said something, but I decided not to. I knew we were all thinking that eating together was different and nice — and also that we weren't going to mention that it was happening.

I opened my milk carton, put my napkin in my lap, and took a good long look at the Stoneybrook Middle School hot lunch.

"What *is* this?" I asked the others.

"Noodles," replied Kristy.

"No, it's poison," said Dawn, who, as usual, was eating a health-food lunch — a container of strawberries, a yogurt with granola mixed in, some dried apple slices, and something I couldn't identify.

"I don't see any noodles here," I said. "Only glue."

"According to the menu, that glue is mushroom and cream sauce," said Claudia.

"Ew," I replied.

"So," said Dawn, "how was everybody's first morning back at school?"

"Fine, Mommy," answered Stacey.

Dawn giggled.

"I have third-period gym with Mrs. Rosenauer," I said. "I hate field hockey, I hate Mrs. Rosenauer, and I hate smelling like gym class for the next five periods. . . . Do I smell like gym class?" I leaned toward Kristy.

She pulled back. "*I'm* not going to smell you. . . . Hey, I just figured something out. You know what the mushroom sauce tastes like? It tastes like a dirty sock that's been left out in the rain and then hidden in a dark closet for three weeks."

The rest of us couldn't decide whether to gag or giggle.

18

Maybe this was why Claudia and Stacey didn't sit with us last year. I changed the subject. "I put the poster of Cam Geary up in my locker this morning," I announced. "I'm going to leave him there all year."

"I want to find a picture of Max Morrison," said Claudia. "That's who I'd like in my locker."

"The boy from 'Out of This World'?" asked Stacey.

Claudia nodded.

I absolutely couldn't eat another bite of the noodles, not after what Kristy had said about the sauce. I gazed around the cafeteria. I saw Trevor Sandbourne, one of Claudia's old boyfriends from last year. I saw the Shillaber twins, who used to sit with Kristy and Dawn and me. They were sitting with the only set of boy twins in school. (For a moment, I thought I had double vision.) I saw Erica and Shawna from homeroom. And then I saw Cam Geary.

I nearly spit out a mouthful of milk.

"Stacey!" I whispered after I'd managed to swallow. "Cam Geary goes to our school! Look!"

All my friends turned to look. "Where? Where?"

"That boy?" said Stacey, smiling. "That's not Cam Geary. That's Logan Bruno. He's new this year. He's in my homeroom and my English class. I talked to him during homeroom. He used to live in Louisville, Kentucky. He has a southern accent."

I didn't care what he sounded like. He was the cutest boy I'd ever seen. He looked exactly like Cam Geary. I was in love with him. And because Stacey already knew so much about him, I was jealous of her. What a way to start the year.

CHAPTER 3

The next day, Friday, was the second day of school, and the end of the first "week" of school. And that night, the members of the Baby-sitters Club held the first meeting of eighth grade. Every last one of us just barely made the meeting on time. Claudia had been working on an art project at school (she loves art and is terrific at it), Dawn had been baby-sitting for the Pikes, Stacey had been at school at a meeting of the dance committee, of which she's vice-president, Kristy had had to wait for Charlie to get home from football practice before he could drive her to the meeting, and I'd been trying to get my weekend homework done before the weekend.

The five of us turned up at five-thirty on the nose, and the phone was ringing as we reached Claudia's room. Dawn grabbed for it, while I tried to find the club record book. Everything was in chaos.

"I love it!" said Kristy when we had settled down.

"You love what?" asked Claudia.

"The excitement, the fast pace."

"You should move to New York," said Stacey.

"No, I'm serious. When things get hectic like this, I get all sorts of great ideas. Summertime is too slow."

"What kinds of great ideas do you get?" asked Dawn, who doesn't know Kristy quite the way the rest of us do. I was pretty sure that Kristy's ideas were going to lead to extra work for the club.

I was right.

"Did you notice the sign in school today?" asked Kristy.

"Kristy, there must have been three thousand signs," replied Claudia. "I saw one for the Remember September Dance, one for the Chess Club, one for cheerleader tryouts, one for class elections — "

"This sign," Kristy interrupted, "was for the PTA. There's going to be a PTA meeting at Stoneybrook Middle School in a few days."

"So?" said Stacey. "PTA stands for Parent Teacher Association. We're kids. It doesn't concern us."

"Oh, yes it does," replied Kristy, "because

where there are *parents* there are *children*, and where there are children, there are parents needing baby-sitters — *us*. That's where we come in."

"*Oh*," I said knowingly. Kristy is so smart. She's such a good businesswoman. That's why she's the president of our club. "More advertising?" I asked.

"Right," replied Kristy.

The phone rang again then, and we stopped to take another job. When we were finished, Kristy continued. "We've got to advertise in school. We'll put up posters where the parents will see them when they come for the meeting."

"Maybe," added Dawn, "we could make up some more fliers and figure out some way for the parents to get them at the meeting. I think it's always better if people have something they can take with them. You know, something to put up on their refrigerator or by their phone."

"Terrific idea," said Kristy, who usually isn't too generous with her praise.

Dawn beamed.

"There's something else," Kristy went on after we'd lined up jobs with the Marshalls and the Perkinses. "When we started this club, it was so that we could baby-sit in our neighborhood, and the four of us — " (Kristy pointed to herself, Claudia, Stacey, and me) " — all lived in the same neighborhood. Then Dawn joined the club, and we found some new clients in her neighborhood. Now *I've* moved, but I, um, I — I haven't, um . . . ."

It was no secret that Kristy had resented moving out of the Thomases' comfortable old split-level and across town to Watson's mansion in his wealthy neighborhood. Of course she liked having a big room with a queen-sized bed and getting treats and being able to have lots of new clothes and stuff. But she'd been living over there for about two months and hadn't made any effort to get to know the people in her new neighborhood. Her brothers had made an effort, and so had her mother, but Kristy claimed that the kids her age were snobs. She and the Thomases' old collie, Louie, kept pretty much to themselves.

I tried to help her through her embarrassment. "It would be good business sense," I pointed out, "to advertise where you live. We should be leaving fliers in the mailboxes over on Edgerstoune Drive and Green House Drive and Bissell Lane."

"And Haslet Avenue and Ober Road, too," said Claudia.

"Right," said Kristy, looking relieved. "After

all, I know Linny and Hannie Papadakis — they're friends of David Michael and Karen. They must need a sitter every now and then. And there are probably plenty of other little kids, too."

"And," said Stacey, adding the one thing the rest of us didn't have the nerve to say, "it might be a good way for you to meet people over there."

Kristy scowled. "Oh, right. All those snobs."

"Kristy, they can't *all* be snobs," said Dawn.

"The ones I met were snobs," Kristy said defiantly. "But what does it matter? We might get some new business."

"Well," I said, "can your mom do some more Xeroxing for us?"

Kristy's mother (who used to be Mrs. Thomas and is now Mrs. Brewer) usually takes one of our fliers to her office and Xeroxes it on the machine there when we need more copies. The machine is so fancy, the fliers almost look as if they'd been printed.

"Sure," replied Kristy, "only this time we'll have to give her some money for the Xerox paper. We've used an awful lot of it. What's in the treasury, Stacey?"

Stacey dumped out the contents of a manila envelope. The money in it is our club dues. We each get to keep anything we earn baby-sitting (we don't try to divide it), but we contribute weekly dues of a dollar apiece to the club. The money pays Charlie for driving Kristy to club meetings and buys any supplies we might need.

"We've got a little over fifteen dollars," said our treasurer.

"Well, I don't know how much Xerox paper costs," said Kristy, "but it's only paper. How many pieces do you think we'll need?"

"A hundred?" I guessed. "A hundred and fifty?"

Kristy took eight dollars out of the treasury. "I'll bring back the change," she said. She looked at her watch. "Boy, only ten more minutes left. This meeting sure went fast."

"We couldn't come early and we can't leave late," said Dawn. "Summer's over."

There was a moment of silence. Even the phone didn't ring.

"I found a picture of Max Morrison," Claudia said finally. "It was in *People* magazine. I'm going to bring it to school on Monday."

"Where is it now?" asked Stacey.

"Here." Claudia took it out of her desk drawer and handed it to Stacey.

"Look at his eyes," said Stacey with a sigh.

"No one's eyes are more amazing than Cam's," I said. "Except maybe Logan Bruno's." I'd seen Logan several more times since lunch the day before. Each time I'd thought he was Cam Geary at first. I wished I'd had an excuse to talk to him, but there was none. We didn't have any classes together, so of course he didn't know who I was.

"Logan Bruno?" Claudia repeated sharply. "Hey, you don't . . . you do! I think you like him, Mary Anne!"

Luckily, I was saved by the ringing of the telephone. I took the call myself, and Stacey ended up with a job at the Newtons'.

By the time I had called Mrs. Newton back and noted the job in our appointment book, my friends were on to another subject.

"Kara Mauricio got a bra yesterday," said Dawn.

I could feel myself blushing. I cleared my throat. "I, um, I, um, I, um — "

"Spit it out, Mary Anne," said Kristy.

"I, um, got a bra yesterday."

"You *did*?" Kristy squeaked.

I nodded. "Dad came home early. He took me to the department store and a saleswoman helped me."

"Was it *awfully* embarrassing?" asked Dawn. "At least my mother helped me get my first one. She kept the saleswomen away."

Kristy was gaping at me. We've both always

been as flat as pancakes, but I'd begun to grow a little over the summer. Kristy must have felt left out. She was the only one of us who didn't wear a bra now.

But suddenly she was all business again. She doesn't like us to get off the subject of the club for *too* long during meetings. "Let's try to get these fliers out next week. Business will really be booming. Who can help me distribute them?"

We looked at our schedules. A few minutes later, the meeting was over. Little did we know what we were getting ourselves into.

CHAPTER 4

"Emergency club meeting at lunch! Tell Kristy!" Claudia flew by me in the hall, her black hair flowing behind her. I caught a whiff of some kind of perfume.

"Wait! What — ?" I started to ask, but Claudia had already been swallowed up by the crowd.

I thought over what she had just said. Emergency meeting . . . *tell Kristy*. That meant Kristy didn't know. But our president was usually the one to call emergency meetings. So who had called it? And what was going on? It was only the beginning of third period. I'd have to wait more than an hour and a half to find out.

I snagged Kristy at the beginning of social studies class. "Emergency meeting at lunch today," I said urgently, leaning across the aisle to her desk.

"Who called it?" Kristy asked immediately,

29

but before I could tell her that I didn't know, our teacher walked in the room.

I snapped back to my desk like a rubber band.

When the class was over, Kristy and I shot out of the room and ran to the cafeteria. We dumped our stuff on our usual table, staking out five chairs at one end. Then we joined the hot-lunch line.

"I wonder what it is today," I said, breathing deeply.

"Smells like steamed rubber in Turtle Wax."

"Kristy, that is so disgusting. What is it really?"

Kristy stood on tiptoe, trying to see over the tops of kids' heads. She jumped up and down a few times. "I don't know," she said finally. "Maybe macaroni and cheese. I can't really see."

She was right. It was macaroni and cheese. Plus limp broccoli, a cup of canned fruit salad, and milk. Kristy and I each bought a chocolate eclair Popsicle, since we don't like macaroni or canned fruit salad. Kristy even considered buying two Popsicles since she doesn't like broccoli, either, but I stopped her. As it was, Dawn was going to die when she saw our lunches.

But when we got to our table we didn't have much time to talk about food. Stacey and Claudia had been not far behind us on the line, and Dawn was already there. So as soon as we had settled down, Kristy said abruptly, "Who called this meeting?"

"I did," said Claudia. "I'm going crazy. I can't handle everything. I've been getting nonstop phone calls ever since that PTA meeting, and since we advertised in your neighborhood, Kristy. I don't mind if people call during our meetings, of course, or once or twice in the evenings, but they're calling all the time. Look at this." She pulled a list out of her notebook. "These calls came last night. And this one came at seven-thirty this morning."

We leaned forward to look at the paper. It was a list of seven names with phone numbers, and notes that said things like "3 kids, 2b, 1g" or "allergic to pets" or "6 yrs, 4 yrs, 3 yrs." None of the names was familiar.

"I would have phoned you guys last night to offer the jobs around as they came in, but that would have meant more than twenty calls. Mom and Dad would have killed me. I'm already behind in my math and English homework." (Claudia is a fabulous artist, but she's not a very good student. In fact, she's only allowed to be in the Baby-sitters Club if she keeps her grades up, which for her means C's.)

"Anyway," Claudia continued, "my social studies teacher assigned a big project this morning, and I guess I just panicked. That was when I called the meeting. I really don't see how I can take art classes, go to school, baby-sit, and be vice-president of the club, too."

Claudia looked near tears, which was unusual for her.

Stacey must have noticed, because she put her hand on Claudia's arm and said, "Hey, Claud, it's okay. Really. We'll work everything out."

"Sure we will," said Dawn.

"We'll take it step by step," added Kristy. She forced down a mouthful of macaroni and cheese. "First things first. What did you tell these people when they called?"

(Kristy really was feeling sorry for Claudia, but you could tell that, underneath, she was thrilled with all the new business we were getting.)

"I told them they would definitely have a sitter, but that I'd have to call them back to say who'd be taking the job."

"Perfect," said Kristy. "That was a good idea."

32

"Excuse me," I interrupted, "but we can save Claudia a little time if the *sitter* calls back. Claudia shouldn't have to do that."

"Right," said Kristy. "Now let's just hope we can schedule all those jobs."

"I brought the record book with me," said Claudia. She pulled it out from between her math book and a reading book. "I know we're not supposed to bring it to school, but I wanted to get this straightened out today, even if we didn't have an actual meeting." (Once, months and months ago, we'd been bringing the record book to school, and Alan Gray, this big pest, had stolen information out of it and used the information to torment Kristy and Claudia.)

"That's all right," said Kristy. "Just be careful with it. Now let's see." She peered at Claudia's list, trying to read her sloppy handwriting. "The first job is on Friday, from six until eight, right?"

Claudia nodded. "A cocktail party."

We turned to the appointment calendar and began assigning jobs. It took some doing but we were able to take care of all of them. Stacey only had to miss one meeting of the dance committee, and Claudia only had to switch around a pottery class.

"Whew," I said, when we were finished.

"You know, that wasn't easy. I'm beginning to wonder if . . ." I paused and unwrapped my Popsicle thoughtfully.

"If what?" asked Dawn.

"If we're in over our heads. Maybe we have *too much* business. What happens if we start getting a lot of jobs we can't handle? What do we tell our clients?"

"Tell them we're busy," suggested Claudia.

"Once or twice, yes. But what if it happens a lot? We shouldn't advertise that we can baby-sit — and then not be able to do it," I pointed out.

"That's true," said Kristy, looking worried for the first time.

"And," I said, starting to feel a little annoyed with her for not having thought about these things in advance, "we definitely shouldn't do any more advertising. We were already pretty busy as it was."

Everyone looked at me. It wasn't the first time I'd criticized Kristy, but I don't do things like that very often.

Kristy bristled. "If you remember, we advertised in my neighborhood so I could get some jobs nearby. Our regular clients would rather have one of *you* sit than *me*, because *somebody* has to drive *me* back to *your* old neighborhood each time *I* have a job there."

Kristy stuck her fork viciously into a spear of broccoli but couldn't bring herself to take a bite.

"Okay, okay," I said grumpily, "but we didn't have to advertise at the PTA meeting." Nobody could argue with that.

After an uncomfortable silence, Claudia, who had calmed down, said practically, "Well, we can't un-advertise, so we better just figure out what to do. We're too busy. How are we going to handle the problem?"

"I've done a lot of baby-sitting," spoke up an unfamiliar male voice.

The five members of the Baby-sitters Club swiveled their heads toward the opposite end of the long table.

"In Louisville," the voice continued. "I've had plenty of experience."

I froze. I froze into an ice statue of Mary Anne. I couldn't even blink my eyes. The voice belonged to Logan Bruno, the wonderful, amazing Cam Geary look-alike.

He really did have a southern accent, too. It sounded as if he'd just said, "In Luevulle. Ah've haid plainy of expuryence."

My friends began to fall all over each other.

"*Really?*" asked Stacey, as if it were the most interesting thing anyone in the history of the world had ever said.

"You're a *sitter*?" exclaimed Claudia, tossing her hair over her shoulder.

"I don't believe it!" cried Dawn.

"Why don't you come talk to us?" asked Kristy.

(I was tongue-tied. My mouth was still frozen.)

Logan was out of his chair in a flash, as if he'd been waiting for the invitation since the beginning of lunch period. The boys he'd been sitting with said (loudly) things like, "Go, Logan!" and "Whoa!" and punched him on the arm, grinning, as he walked to our end of the table. He sat down next to me.

If anything should have made me melt, it was Logan, but I was frozen solid. I couldn't even turn my head to look into his dark eyes. I was dying.

"Hi," said Logan lightly, as if he were used to plopping himself down with a bunch of strange girls. "I'm Logan Bruno." He looked around at us. "Oh, hi, Stacey," he added, and a little wave of jealousy washed over me.

"Hi," replied Stacey. "Logan, these are my friends." She pointed to each of us in turn. "Claudia Kishi, Dawn Schafer, Kristy Thomas, and Mary Anne Spier."

Logan smiled warmly at me, but I couldn't return the smile.

"I didn't mean to eavesdrop," he said, "but I did overhear you say that you were sort of in a jam."

"We are," said Kristy. "See, we run this business called the Baby-sitters Club." Kristy explained how the club had started and how it works. "So you've really done a lot of sitting?" she added when she'd finished.

Logan nodded. "I've got a nine-year-old sister and a five-year-old brother, and I sit for them a lot. And I used to baby-sit for our neighbors, too, when we lived in Louisville. I haven't found anyone to sit for here, though." Logan paused. "I've even taken care of babies. I don't like changing diapers, but . . ." He shrugged as if to say, "It's just part of the job."

"How late can you stay out at night?" asked Kristy.

(We were all staring at Logan. Not one of us could take her eyes off him.)

"Oh, I don't know. I guess about ten-thirty on a weeknight. Maybe midnight on Fridays and Saturdays."

"Super!" exclaimed Stacey.

We all nodded. (I was thawing out.)

"Want to come to our next meeting?" asked Kristy abruptly. "I mean, just to see what the club's all about?"

"Sure," replied Logan. Kristy told him when it was, and then he unfolded his long legs from under the cafeteria table and returned to the boys he'd been sitting with.

"Way to go!" exclaimed one of the boys.

"Yeah," added another. "All those girls. Are you ever lucky."

Suddenly I found myself beaming. The boys were *jealous* of Logan because of *us*. Not only that, Logan was going to attend our next meeting!

CHAPTER 5

Needless to say, I was a nervous wreck before the next meeting of the Baby-sitters Club. I was sitting for Jamie and Lucy Newton, and Mrs. Newton had said she'd be back between five and five-thirty. When she showed up at 4:45, I had never been so glad to make an early getaway. I ran home, locked myself in the bathroom, and studied myself critically in the mirror. My hair is mouse-brown, but it looks okay if I let it flow down over my shoulders. My dad used to be really, really strict, and he made me wear it in braids, but not anymore. Now I wear it loose. If I just brush it and leave it alone, it ripples nicely, kind of as if I'd had a body wave, which I haven't.

I brushed my hair one hundred times. I don't have any makeup, but I do have some jewelry, so I put on a pair of small hoop earrings and a gold chain bracelet that used to belong to my mother. Then I took off the sweat shirt I'd been wearing and put on a bright vest over a short-sleeved white blouse. I looked . . . not bad.

When it was only five-fifteen I ran to Claudia's. I was not the first one there. We were all excited about Logan Bruno. I met Stacey and Kristy at the front door, and when we reached our club headquarters, we found Claudia and Dawn already lying on the bed. They were eating popcorn.

"I can't wait!" Claudia was squealing.

"I know," said Dawn. "He is *so* ado*ra*ble."

They were talking about Logan, of course.

Kristy practically bounced into the director's chair. I trailed after her, the last one into the room.

"Hey!" exclaimed Claudia. "You look nice, Mary Anne!"

"Thanks," I replied, blushing.

There was dead silence.

I didn't think I looked too different, but I must have, because all at once, everyone realized what I was doing.

"It's for Logan, isn't it," said Stacey softly, not even asking a question. She knew she was right.

"Of course not," I replied.

"Oh, come on, Mary Anne. You can tell *us*. We're your friends."

But just then the doorbell rang. Claudia sprang off her bed and dashed out of the room, through the hall, and down the stairs. A few seconds later, we heard the front door open. Then we heard two voices, one male and one female.

Logan had arrived.

Now, I don't know about Claudia, but there has never been a boy in *my* bedroom. (I mean, a boy who counts. Kristy's little brother doesn't count.) What would a boy have thought of my horse books and Snowman, my white teddy bear? What would a boy have thought of my lacy pillow sham or Lila, my antique doll?

I looked around Claudia's room. There were the four of us, the bowl of popcorn, and this rag doll of Claudia's named Lennie. Before Claudia and Logan reached the top of the stairs, I stuffed Lennie under the bed. Then I checked Claudia's bureau to make sure there was no underwear sticking out of drawers or anything. Her room wasn't too neat, but it seemed safe.

I cleared a spot on the floor for Logan.

I cleared it next to me.

"Hey, everybody," drawled Logan's familiar voice.

There he was, framed in Claudia's doorway.

He looked more handsome than ever.

Claudia was settling herself on the bed again. "Come on in," she said. "Pull up a patch of floor." She began to giggle.

Logan grinned and sat next to me. "Mary Anne, right?" he said.

I nodded. But my tongue felt as if someone had poured Elmer's glue on it and then covered it with sawdust.

"Let me make sure I have this right," Logan went on. He looked at each of us in turn. "Claudia, um, Kristy . . . Dawn?" (Dawn nodded.) "And Stacey. You, I know."

Stacey smiled charmingly.

"So," said Logan. "What do we do here?"

(I loved his southern accent. I *loved* it!)

Kristy, Claudia, Stacey, and Dawn all began to talk.

"We answer the phone."

"People call in."

"We find the record book."

"We look in the treasury."

Logan glanced at me. "What do *you* do?"

The glue and sawdust just wouldn't go away. I tried clearing my throat. Ahem. *Ahem.* "I — " I croaked. "I, um — "

Stacey handed me the record book. "She's our secretary," she spoke up. "Mary Anne sets up our appointments."

"Oh," said Logan. "I see." But he gave me a funny look.

At last the phone rang. The five of us jumped for it. Dawn got there first. "Hello, Baby-sitters Club," she said. "Oh, hi! . . . Yes. . . . Monday? . . . Okay, I'll get back to you." She hung up. "That was Mrs. Perkins. She has a doctor's appointment next Monday afternoon. She needs someone to watch Myriah and Gabbie from three-thirty till five-thirty." Dawn turned to Logan. "The Perkinses live right across the street. They've got two little girls, and Mrs. Perkins is expecting another baby. That's why she has to go to the doctor."

"Okay," said Logan.

"Well, who's free?" asked Dawn, looking at me.

Why was she — ? Oh, right. The appointment book. I picked it up, dropped it, picked it up, and dropped it again. Finally Logan handed it to me. I turned to the appointment calendar.

"What day did you say?" I asked Dawn.

"Next Monday."

"Um . . . I'm free and Claudia's free."

"You take it," said Claudia. "I've got to have a little time for my pottery."

"Thanks," I murmured, and penciled myself in.

Dawn called Mrs. Perkins back to tell her who the sitter would be.

"And that's how we work things," said Kristy to Logan as Dawn was hanging up.

"That's great," said Logan. "And you really get a lot of calls?"

As if in answer to his question, the phone rang three more times — Mrs. Pike, Mrs. Prezzioso, and a new client, a Mr. Ohdner, who needed a sitter for his two daughters. We assigned the jobs — but just barely. Claudia and Stacey were now busy with something every afternoon after school next week.

Claudia passed around the popcorn. Suddenly she burst out laughing. "You know what this reminds me of?" she said, patting the bowl.

"What?" we all asked.

"You know Dorianne Wallingford? Well, last weekend Pete Black takes her to the movies, and about halfway through, he reaches around behind her and snaps her br — " Claudia stopped abruptly.

I knew what she'd been about to say. *Her bra strap.* (Pete was always doing that, just to be mean.) Claudia had almost said *bra strap* in front of a *boy*.

Claudia began to blush. So did I. So did everyone in the room including Logan.

It was an awful moment. Logan tried to cover up. "Here, have some," he said, passing me the popcorn.

I don't know how it ended up upside-down, but it did.

"Oh, no!" I cried. I scrambled around, trying to put the kernels back in the bowl.

Logan and Stacey leaned over to help and knocked heads.

Somebody better do something fast, I thought. Bring up a new subject . . . anything.

Claudia must have been a mind-reader because she turned to Logan then and said, "What was your worst baby-sitting experience ever?"

"Well," said Logan (only it sounded like *way-ull*), "let me see. There was the time Tina Lawrence flushed one of her father's neckties down the toilet." (We laughed.) "And there was the time my brother got into Mom's lipsticks and colored the bathroom pink and red. But I think the worst time was when I was sitting for this little kid named Elliott. His mother was trying to toilet-train him and she showed me where his special potty was and everything. All morning after she left I kept asking Elliott if he needed to go, and all morning he kept saying, 'No, no, no.' So finally I took him into the bathroom and . . ."

"And what?" I dared to ask.

Logan was blushing again. "I just realized. I can't say that part. . . ."

"Oh," I said lamely.

A horrible silence fell over Claudia's room.

I looked at my watch. Ten more minutes before the meeting was over.

"Anyone want some soda?" asked Claudia.

"I do!" we all said instantly.

Claudia got to her feet. Logan jumped up and followed her out the door. "I'll help you," he said.

As soon as they were downstairs, the other members of the Baby-sitters Club began moaning horribly. "Oh, this is so em*bar*rassing," cried Stacey.

"I *know*," said Kristy. "Can we really ask a boy to join the club? I didn't think about stuff like this. We're not even having a regular meeting. At least, it sure doesn't feel like it. We're hardly talking about club stuff at all."

My head was spinning. I wanted Logan to be in the club, but if he joined — would I ever speak again? Or would I have a sawdust-covered tongue for eternity? And would we ever have another nice, normal, businesslike meeting?

When Claudia and Logan returned, Logan sat down next to me and handed me a glass of Diet Coke, while Claudia handed glasses to the others. He smiled at me. "What was *your* worst baby-sitting experience?" he asked.

I'd had several pretty bad ones, but they all flew right out of my head. "Oh . . . I don't, um, know," I mumbled.

Logan nodded. What could he say to that? He turned to Kristy the chatterbox.

"Stacey told me the club was all your idea," he said.

Kristy nodded. "It just sort of came to me one evening," she replied loftily.

Ring, ring.

Kristy reached over and picked up the phone, somehow managing not to take her eyes off Logan. (The things a cute boy did to our club. . . .)

"Hello, Baby-sitters Club." We all listened to Kristy's end of the conversation. From the questions she was asking, I could tell the caller was another new client. When she hung up the phone, she said, "Okay, that was someone named Mrs. Rodowsky. She has three boys. They're nine, seven, and four. They live way over on Reilly Lane. She picked up one of our fliers at the PTA meeting."

"Reilly Lane?" interrupted Logan. "Isn't that near where I live?"

"Yup," said Kristy. "A few streets over. And

I'd like you to take the job. They'd be good clients for you, living nearby with three boys and all. The only thing is — I hope you don't mind — I'd kind of like one of us to, you know, see you in action first. I mean, I know you've done a lot of baby-sitting, but . . ."

"That's okay," said Logan. "I understand."

"Oh, good," said Kristy. "Well then, even though there's only going to be one of the Rodowsky boys to sit for next week — the seven-year-old — I want two baby-sitters to go on the job. Logan and someone who's free. Mary Anne?"

For once I was on my toes. I picked up the record book. "What day?" I asked.

"Thursday. Three-thirty till six."

I looked at Thursday. I gasped. Then I cleared my throat. "I'm the only one free," I croaked.

Logan smiled at me. "I guess we've got the job," he said.

I nearly fainted. "I guess so," I replied.

CHAPTER 6

Kristy had called Mrs. Rodowsky back and explained why two sitters would be coming for the price of one. Mrs. Rodowsky had been very impressed and said we sounded responsible and mature.

Maybe that's how we had *sounded*, but I *felt* like I had spaghetti for bones. I'd felt that way ever since the club meeting. Now it was the day Logan and I were supposed to baby-sit.

I met him in front of the Rodowskys' at 3:25. As soon as I saw him, my legs and arms felt all floppy. The sawdust returned to my tongue. It was like this every time I got within a mile of him. Or even if someone mentioned his name.

"Hi!" Logan called.

I was going to have to shape up. I really was. This was a job. This was business. I couldn't have spaghetti-bones and a sawdust-tongue while I was trying to baby-sit.

"Hi!" I replied brightly. I smiled. (There. That hadn't been so bad.)

"Ready?" asked Logan. He smiled, too.

"I hope so," I said. "How much trouble can one little kid be?" (Obviously, I wasn't thinking straight. Otherwise, Jenny Prezzioso would have come to mind, and I'd have kept my mouth shut.)

Logan and I walked to the Rodowskys' front door and Logan rang the bell. It was answered by a tall, thin woman wearing blue jeans and a jean jacket. She didn't look like most mothers I knew.

"Hello," she said. "You must be Mary Anne and Logan. I'm Mariel Rodowsky. Call me Mariel. Come on in." She held the door open for us.

Logan and I stepped inside.

"Jackie!" Mrs. Rodowsky called. (I just couldn't think of her as Mariel. It's hard to call adults by their first names.) "Your sitters are here."

We heard footsteps on a staircase, and in a moment, a red-haired, red-cheeked, freckle-faced little boy bounded into the front hall.

"This is Jackie," said Mrs. Rodowsky. "Jackie,

this is Mary Anne, and this is Logan."

"Hi," Logan and I said at the same time.

"Hi," replied Jackie. "I got a grasshopper. Wanna see him?"

"Honey," his mother said, "let me talk to Logan and Mary Anne first. Then you can show them the grasshopper." Mrs. Rodowsky turned back to us. "Jackie's brothers have lessons at the Y today and I have a meeting. I've left the number of both the YMCA and the Stoneybrook Historical Society by the telephone. We should be back at six or a little before. I guess that's it. Jackie's used to sitters. You shouldn't have any problems. Just . . . just keep your eye on him, okay?"

"Oh, sure," said Logan. "That's what we're here for."

"Great," said Mrs. Rodowsky with a smile.

(One point for Logan, I thought. He was good with parents.)

A few minutes later, Mrs. Rodowsky left with two other redheaded boys.

Jackie began jumping on the couch in the rec room.

"Boing! Boing! Boing!" he cried. "I'm a basketball! Watch me make a basket!"

Jackie took a terrific leap off the couch, his knees tucked under his chin as if he were going to cannonball into a swimming pool. Logan caught him just before he crashed into the piano.

I'm not sure what I would have done if *I'd* caught Jackie, but Logan raised him in the air and shouted, "Yes, it's the deciding basket, fans! The Rodowsky Rockets have won the Interstellar Championship, and it's all due to Jackie, the human basketball!" Then he carried him away from the couch and the piano. (Another point for Logan.)

I hung back. This was really Logan's job, not mine. I was just along to watch.

Jackie giggled. He squirmed out of Logan's arms. "I gotta show you guys my grasshopper," he said. "His name is Elizabeth."

"You've got a grasshopper named Elizabeth?" said Logan.

"A *boy* grasshopper?" I added.

"Yup," replied Jackie. "I'll go get him for you. Be right back."

Jackie dashed up the stairs.

Logan glanced at me. "Whoa," he said. "That kid's got energy."

I nodded, feeling shy.

Logan wandered into the living room and waited. I followed him.

"Mr. and Mrs. Rodowsky must have their hands full," Logan commented.

"Probably," I managed to reply.

"Maybe they'll need sitters often," he added. "I wouldn't mind."

I gazed at the walls of the Rodowskys' living room. They were covered with the boys' artwork, professionally framed. Logan wandered over to one of the pictures — a house formed by a red square with a black triangle sitting on top of it. A green line below indicated grass, a blue line above indicated sky. A yellow sun peeked out of the corner.

"Well, what do you know," said Logan. "We've got a painting just like this at our house. Only it says *Logan* at the bottom, not *Jackie*. And all these years I thought it was an original."

I giggled. We had one of them, too. Why couldn't I say so? I looked at the other paintings. Logan picked up a magazine.

"It's, um, it's — it's taking Jackie an awfully long time to — " I was stammering, when suddenly we heard a noise from upstairs.

KER-THUD!

The crash was followed by a cry.

Logan and I glanced at each other. Then we ran for the stairs. Logan reached them first. We dashed to the second floor.

"Jackie!" Logan bellowed. "Where are you?"

"Ow! . . . I'm in the bathroom."

Logan made a sharp left and skidded to a stop. I was right behind him. Jackie was sitting on the floor. The shower curtain was in a heap around him, and the rod that had held the curtain was sticking crazily out of the tub.

My first thought was to run to Jackie, give him a hug, and find out what had happened. But I hung back. This was Logan's job.

"Are you hurt?" exclaimed Logan.

"Nope," said Jackie. He stood up.

"Well, what happened?"

(So far, so good, I thought. But as far as I was concerned, Logan had made one mistake. After letting Jackie go upstairs alone, he had let far too much time go by. He should have checked on him after just a couple of minutes. Minus one point.)

Jackie looked a little sheepish. "Today in gym we were exercising. We were climbing ropes and chinning on these bars — "

"And you thought you'd try chinning on the curtain rod," Logan interrupted.

"Yeah," said Jackie. "How did you know?"

"I did it myself once."

Jackie nodded. (What was this? Some sort of boy's ritual I'd never heard of?) "I stood on the edge of the tub," said Jackie, "grabbed onto the rod, and as soon as I pulled myself up, the bar crashed down!"

"When I did it, I had to have six stitches taken in my lip," said Logan. "Look, here's the scar."

I shook my head. Logan hadn't checked Jackie for bumps or cuts, and he hadn't told him not to try chinning again. I waited a few moments longer. The boys were discussing gym class catastrophes. It was time to break in.

"Um, Jackie," I said, "I'm glad you're not hurt, but you better let us check you over, just in case."

Logan looked at me in surprise. "Oh, yeah," he said. "Good idea."

I checked Jackie's arms and legs while Logan rehung the curtain rod. A bruise was already coming out on one of Jackie's knees, but it didn't look too bad. "Now let me feel your head," I said. "You wouldn't want a big goose egg, would you?"

"Goose egg?" repeated Jackie, giggling.

Logan smiled. "I should have thought of this, Mary Anne," he said. "Sorry. I'm glad you're here."

"Thanks," I said, and actually smiled. (*I* was glad *he* was there.) I decided the talk about not chinning could wait until later.

Jackie's head seemed fine. The three of us went downstairs. "I need some juice," Jackie announced. He made a beeline for the refrigerator and took out a jar of grape juice.

"Better let me pour," said Logan. (Score another point.)

"No, no. I can do it." Jackie got a paper cup and filled it to the brim. "I'll have it in the living room," he said, and before we knew what was happening, he ran out of the kitchen, tripped, and spilled the entire cup of juice on the living room carpet.

"Oh, no," I moaned.

But Logan kept his head. For one thing, the carpet was dark blue, so the juice didn't show — much. Logan sent Jackie into the kitchen for paper towels. He got busy with water, soap, and finally a little soda water. When he was done, the rug was smelly and damp, but he assured me there wouldn't be a stain.

I was pretty impressed.

"Hey!" said Jackie. "I never showed you Elizabeth." He started up the stairs.

"We'll come with you," said Logan hastily. (I was relieved. He was doing okay after all.)

We followed Jackie into his bedroom. He removed a jar from the windowsill. "This is Elizabeth," he said softly. He reached into the jar, let Elizabeth crawl onto a finger, pulled his hand up — and found that his hand was stuck.

No matter how we pulled and twisted, Logan and I couldn't get the jar off Jackie's hand.

"Do you think we could break it without cutting Jackie?" I asked.

Logan frowned and shook his head. "I've got a better idea," he said. He went downstairs and returned with a tub of margarine. A few seconds later, Jackie's greasy hand was out of the jar.

"Good thinking!" I exclaimed.

Logan grinned. "What was it you said just before we rang the doorbell this afternoon?"

"I said . . . oh, yeah." (I'd said, "How much trouble can one little kid be?" but I didn't want to repeat that in front of Jackie.)

Before Mrs. Rodowsky returned, Jackie managed to fall off his bicycle, rip his jeans, and later to make *me* fall over backward into Logan's arms. (Sigh.) I felt that Logan had earned every penny he was paid. I was really proud of the job he'd done — and I was glad the Rodowskys were going to be mostly *his* clients.

As Logan and I crossed the Rodowskys' lawn, the front door safely closed behind us, Logan said, "I'll never forget the look on your face when Jackie spilled that juice."

"I'll never forget the look on your face when the jar got stuck on his hand!"

"And," Logan added, "I'll never forget the

look on your face when Jackie knocked you into me."

I blushed furiously.

"Oh, no," said Logan quickly. "It was a *nice* look. Really nice. You know, you have a pretty smile."

I do?

I was melting, melting away. I was turning into a wonderful Mary Anne puddle. And all because of Logan.

CHAPTER 7

Friday

I love ~~mose Myjih~~ Myriah and Gabbie. I really do. But that Chewy. What a dog! This afternoon I was suposed to hav a nise easy siting job at the Perkins but Chewy caused so many problems I can't believe it. Mrs. Perkins asked Gabie and me to meet Myriah when the bus from the comuty center ¢ droped her off we did but we broght Chewy whith us. What a mistake! Heres a tip for everyone in the club. Never ever let Chewey out of the bake yard! Im not kidding !!!!

Claudia really wasn't kidding. After her experience, no one will ever let Chewbacca Perkins loose again — unless we're told to walk him or something. He's a sweet, lovable dog, but he's so *big*. And he gets so ex*cit*ed.

Claudia went to the Perkinses' house right after school on Thursday. Gabbie answered the doorbell. "Hi, Claudee Kishi!" she cried, jumping up and down.

"Hiya, Gabbers." Claudia let herself inside.

Gabbie held up her arms. "Toshe me up, please."

Claudia picked her up and gave her a squeeze. Gabbie is very huggable. "Hi, Mrs. Perkins," she called.

Mrs. Perkins was frantically folding laundry in the living room. "Oh, Claudia, thank goodness you're here. It's been one of those days. The dryer just broke, although not till after I'd done this load, we have a leak in the bathroom, and Gabbie spent all morning gluing stickers to her bedroom door."

"Want to see, Claudee Kishi? My door is very beautiful."

"You did a nice job, sweetie," said Mrs. Perkins, struggling with a sheet, "but stickers don't go on doors. They go on paper."

60

"My door is very beautiful," Gabbie repeated, looking serious.

"Where's Myriah?" asked Claudia.

"Oh, she's at the Community Center." Mrs. Perkins stood up, carrying a pile of folded clothes. "She takes Creative Theater there on Thursdays after kindergarten. The Community Center bus will drop her off at the corner of Bradford and Elm. I need you and Gabbie to meet her there at four, okay?"

"Sure," replied Claudia.

"I'll be back a little after five. I have a checkup with the doctor, and then I'm going to drop by a friend's house. Both numbers are posted on the refrigerator. So's the number of the Community Center, just in case."

"Okay. Where's Chewy?"

Mrs. Perkins smiled. "You missed his galloping feet? He's out in the backyard. He's fine there."

Chewbacca is a black Labrador retriever. He has more energy than all eight Pike kids plus Jackie Rodowsky put together. The Perkinses have fenced in the entire backyard for him so he has a big safe area to run around in.

Mrs. Perkins checked her watch. "Oh, I'm going to be late! Claudia, could you carry these clothes upstairs for me? Leave them anywhere. By the way, the girls can have a snack later. Myriah is usually starving by the time she gets home from the center."

"Okay," said Claudia. "See you later. We're going to have lots of fun. Right, Gabbers?"

"Right, Claudee Kishi."

Mrs. Perkins rushed off. Gabbie helped Claudia carry the clothes upstairs. When they'd finished, she took Claudia by the hand and led her to her bedroom.

"See my beautiful door?" she said.

Claudia smiled. It really was covered with stickers — wildlife stickers with gummed backs — from the floor to as high up as Gabbie could reach, which wasn't very high.

"You must have worked hard," said Claudia.

Gabbie nodded. "Yes," she agreed. "I did."

Claudia wondered what she would have done if Gabbie were her little girl. The door wasn't ruined, but it would take a lot of work to scrape off the stickers. Gabbie didn't think she had done anything wrong, though. She had only wanted to make her door "beautiful." It must be hard to be a parent, Claudia thought.

"Well," said Claudia, "what do you want to do? We don't have to meet your sister for a while."

"I want to . . ." Gabbie frowned. "I want to play with Cindy Jane." (Cindy Jane is an old Cabbage Patch doll. Myriah says her name is really Caroline Eunice.)

Gabbie found the doll. She placed her in a baby carriage and wheeled her around the house, singing to her. By the time she got bored, Claudia was ready to meet Myriah.

"Let's go, Gabbers," she said. "It's almost four o'clock. Your sister will be getting off the bus soon."

Claudia and Gabbie left the house through the garage door. As they started down the driveway, Chewy barked at them from the backyard.

"Poor Chewy," said Claudia, turning around. "I bet you want to come with us, don't you?"

Chewy was standing on his hind legs, front paws resting on the fence. He whined pitifully.

"What do you think, Gabbie?" Claudia asked. "Should we bring him with us? He looks like he'd enjoy a walk."

"Mommy doesn't walk him to the bus stop," Gabbie replied.

"But we could. Do you know where his leash is?"

"Yes," said Gabbie. "It's in the mud room."

Sure enough, Claudia found a fancy red leash hanging from a hook in the "mud room." It said *Chewy* all over it in white letters.

"Okay, boy. Here you go," Claudia murmured as she clipped the leash on Chewy's collar.

Chewy began wriggling with joy — tail first, then hindquarters. The wriggle slowly worked its way along his body until he was yapping and wagging and grinning. If he could talk, he would have been saying, "Oh, boyo, boyo, boy! What a great day! Are you guys really taking me for a walk? Huh? Are you? Oh, boyo, boyo, boy!"

Claudia grinned. "I wish *we* had a dog," she told Gabbie.

"Daddy says having Chewy is like having three dogs," remarked Gabbie.

Now that should have told Claudia something, but both she and Chewy were too excited for Claudia to pay much attention.

"Okay, boy. Here we go." Claudia took Chewy's leash in one hand, and Gabbie's hand in the other. They set off with a jerk as Chewy bounded out of the yard.

"Whoa, Chewy, slow down!" cried Claudia. She held him back, but he strained and pulled on the leash, whuffling and sniffing at everything he saw — rocks, patches of grass, cracks in the sidewalk.

Claudia and Gabbie passed a work crew repairing the road and reached the corner where they were to meet Myriah. A few moments later the yellow Community Center bus pulled to a stop.

"There's your sister!" Claudia told Gabbie.

"Where?" Gabbie stood on her tiptoes and craned her neck around.

"There. Look in the window."

Myriah was waving from a seat near the front, but Gabbie exclaimed, "I still can't see her."

So Claudia picked her up, dropping Chewy's leash as she did so. "Uh-oh," said Claudia.

As the bus door opened, Chewy bounded away. Claudia made a grab for the leash and missed. Myriah stepped off the bus then and Chewy ran to her with a joyous woof. But he didn't stop when he reached her. He snatched her schoolbag out of her hand and gallumphed away.

"Chewy!" Myriah screamed.

"Chewy!" Claudia and Gabbie screamed.

The bus drove off.

"Claudia!" cried Myriah. "He took my bag. Get him! There's a note from my teacher in there! And a permission slip and my workbook pages with stars on them!"

Chewy was halfway down the block by then, his leash trailing behind him. He tore along, every now and then looking over his shoulder at Claudia and the girls with a doggie grin, as if the chase were a big game.

"My bag's going to be all slobbery!" said Myriah.

"Well, come on, you guys!" shouted Claudia. She took off after Chewy, with the girls behind her.

Chewy ran into the Newtons' yard.

"Look out, Mrs. Newton!" yelped Claudia.

Mrs. Newton was working in a flower bed, with Jamie and Lucy playing nearby. When she saw Chewy, she dashed to Lucy and picked her up, whisking her out of Chewy's path.

"Help us catch Chewy, Jamie!" called Myriah.

Jamie joined the chase.

Chewy ran into Claudia's yard. Mimi, Claudia's grandmother, was taking a teetery stroll down the front walk.

"Look out, Mimi!" cried Claudia.

Mimi stepped aside, but actually tried to grab Myriah's bag as Chewy flew by.

She missed.

"Thanks anyway, Mimi!" Myriah shouted.

Chewy gallumphed on, and Charlotte Johanssen, Stacey's favorite baby-sitting charge, rounded a corner. She saw Chewy coming at her full speed.

"Aughh!" she screamed.

Chewy put on the brakes to avoid her.

"Get the bag!" yelled Claudia.

And Charlotte did just that — but then Chewy sped up and tore away again.

"Oh, *thank* you," Myriah said breathlessly to Charlotte. "This bag is full of important stuff."

Well, the bag was back but Chewy wasn't. Claudia didn't know what to do. She couldn't catch Chewy, so she simply returned to the Perkinses' with Myriah and Gabbie, and waited. Mrs. Perkins would be home around five. At 4:40, Claudia began to feel very worried. At 4:45, she was a bundle of nerves. At 4:50, the doorbell rang.

Claudia answered it. A workman wearing blue overalls was standing on the steps. "Hi," he said. "I'm fixing the road." He jerked his thumb in the direction of the repair crew that Claudia and Gabbie had passed earlier.

"Yes?" said Claudia curiously.

"Well," the man continued, "I really like

your dog. He's very nice and all, but he won't give me my cones back."

Claudia didn't have the faintest idea what the man was talking about.

"Go look in your backyard," the man said.

Claudia left him at the door and ran through the house. She looked out the kitchen window. There was Chewy dragging a big orange plastic roadmarker over to a pile that he had gathered by the swingset. Claudia snuck outside and trapped Chewy on his next trip to the road crew. The workman took his cones back. Mrs. Perkins came home. Claudia told her what had happened while she was gone. But she wasn't sure Mrs. Perkins believed her. Claudia couldn't blame her.

CHAPTER 8

"Ahem, ahem. Please come to order," said Kristy.

Every now and then our president becomes zealous and tries to run our club meetings according to parliamentary procedure.

We couldn't come to order, though. The rest of us were still laughing over the story of Chewy and the orange cones.

"Well, I guess I'll just have to decide about Logan by myself," said Kristy.

That brought us to attention. I'd been sprawled on Claudia's bed. I sat up straight. Stacey and Dawn stopped giggling. Claudia even forgot to look around her room for hidden junk food.

"Okay," said Kristy more casually. "We've all talked to Logan. He's come to one meeting. And now, he's gone on a job. Mary Anne, what did you think?"

"Well, for awhile, I wasn't too impressed,"

I admitted. I told them about the shower rod incident. "But he was great with Mrs. Rodowsky, and getting along with the parents is always important. Plus, he's good in a crisis, really levelheaded, and he's good at distracting kids from things they shouldn't be doing." I added the stories about the grape juice, the stuck jar, and the cannonball off the couch.

"Jackie Rodowsky sounds like a real handful," said Stacey incredulously when I was finished.

"Well, he is, but he doesn't mean to be," I told her. "He's just sort of accident-prone. He's really a nice little kid. You could tell he loved Elizabeth. He was very gentle with him."

"Would you say Logan is a responsible baby-sitter?" asked Kristy. "Could we safely send him to our clients?"

"Definitely," I replied, and I wasn't just thinking of being in love when I said that.

"And we all like him, right?" Kristy went on.

"Yes," we agreed. It was unanimous.

Kristy paused. "But do we want to ask him to be a member of the club?"

Silence.

Even I couldn't say yes to that. I had visions of one uncomfortable meeting after another, each of us trying not to talk about boys, trying not to mention things that were unmentionable, and of poor Lennie the rag doll spending the rest of her days under Claudia's bed.

"I thought so," said Kristy after awhile.

We all began to talk at once:

"I really like Logan."

"Logan's great, but . . ."

"The Rodowskys need Logan."

"I was so embarrassed when . . ."

"Logan was so embarrassed when . . ."

"Okay, okay, okay," said Kristy, holding up her hands. "We've got a little problem here."

The phone rang and I answered it. I heard Mrs. Rodowsky's voice on the other end. "Hi," I greeted her. "How's Jackie?"

"Oh, he's fine. As a matter of fact, he hasn't stopped talking about you and Logan. He had a wonderful time with you. And Mr. Rodowsky and I need a sitter next Saturday night for all three boys. We have tickets to a play in Stamford."

"Okay," I said. "I'll have to check our schedule. I'll call you back in a few minutes." I hung up the phone. "That was Mrs. Rodowsky," I told the others. "She needs a sitter next Saturday." I flipped through the record book to the appointment calendar.

"Who's free?" asked Kristy, leaning forward.

"Uh-oh. No one is," I said.

Kristy exhaled noisily.

"What about Logan?" asked Dawn.

"He really isn't a club member yet," Kristy replied.

"He might be free, though," spoke up Stacey.

"But we can't count on that," said Kristy. "And I don't want to start recommending him if he isn't a club member."

I didn't quite follow Kristy's reasoning on that, but I said, "Well, look, I'm busy that Saturday, but I'm not baby-sitting. These clients of Dad's are going to be visiting. He asked me to go out to dinner with them, but I know it's going to be really boring. I think Dad will let me baby-sit if I explain that we're in a tight spot. That way, I can call Mrs. Rodowsky back now, tell her that either Logan or I will be able to sit, and after we decide what to do about letting Logan in the club, we'll tell her which one of us will be coming."

"Fine," agreed Kristy.

So I did that, and then Kristy said, "Okay, what about Logan?"

We all looked at each other. We just couldn't decide what to say.

Finally Claudia found some Doritos and

passed the bag around. The munching didn't help us make a decision, though.

"Well, look," said Stacey after awhile. "I think Logan was embarrassed at the meeting, too. Maybe he doesn't even want to be part of the club."

"He went on the sitting job, though," I pointed out. "He must still be interested."

"He probably felt like he had to go," said Claudia.

"All right," said Kristy. "Here's what I think we should do. Call Logan and be completely honest with him. Tell him we think he's a great baby-sitter, but that the meeting was a little . . . awkward. Then just see what he says."

"I think that's a good plan," said Stacey. "Who should call him?"

"Well," Kristy said, and very slowly four heads turned toward me. Kristy, Claudia, Stacey, and Dawn were grinning mischievously.

"Me?" I exclaimed.

"Who else?" said Kristy.

"Well, at least let me call him in private."

I left the meeting a few minutes early that day. I wanted to make sure I got done with the phone call before Dad came home from work. It was going to be a tight squeeze. Our meetings are over at six, Dad usually gets home between 6:15 and 6:30, and I'm responsible for having dinner started by then.

If I'd had any extra time at all, I would have delayed calling Logan. I might have put it off for a day, a week, a decade. But I was pressed. And I had an entire business to be responsible to.

I used the phone upstairs, just in case Dad should come home early. I sat in the armchair in his room holding a slip of paper in one hand. Logan's number was written on the paper. I took ten deep breaths. I was trying to calm down, but the breaths made me dizzy. I think I was hyperventilating. I stretched out on Dad's bed until I'd recovered.

All right. Okay. Time to dial.

K-L-five-one-zero-one-eight.

Maybe no one was home. Maybe the line would be busy.

Ring.

"Hello?"

Someone answered right away! I was so flustered I almost hung up.

"Hello?" said the voice again. It was a woman.

I cleared my throat. "Um, hello, this is Mary Anne Spier. Is Logan there, please?"

"Just a moment."

There was a pause followed by some muffled sounds. Then, "Hello?"

"Hi, Logan. This is Mary Anne." My voice was shaking.

"Hey," he said. "What's up?"

"Well, we just had a club meeting," I began, "and we agreed that you're a good sitter, someone, you know, we could recommend to our clients. So about joining the club — "

Logan interrupted me just as I was getting to the most difficult thing I had to tell him. "Mary Anne," he said, "I don't know how to say this, but I — I've decided not to join the Baby-sitters Club."

He *had*? A funny little shiver ran down my back. I wanted to ask him why he'd decided that, but I was afraid. Hadn't we laughed together as we'd left the Rodowskys'? Hadn't Logan told me I had a pretty smile? Had I misunderstood everything?

I must have been quiet longer than I'd thought because Logan said, "Mary Anne? Are you still there?"

I found my voice. "Yes."

"I was wondering something, though. Would you come to the Remember September Dance with me?"

(Would I?!)

"Sure!" I exclaimed, without thinking of all

sorts of important things, such as I don't like crowds of people, I don't know how to dance, and my father might not even let me go. "I'll have to check with my father, though," I added hastily.

I got off the phone feeling giddy. Logan liked me! Out of all the girls in Stoneybrook Middle School, he'd asked *me* to the Remember September Dance. I couldn't believe it. I'd have to learn to dance, of course, but no problem.

I was so excited, I just had to call someone and spread the news. I called Dawn. When we got off the phone, I started dinner. I was walking on air. I was almost able to ignore the voice in the back of my mind that kept saying, "Why doesn't Logan want to join our club?"

CHAPTER 9

Tuesday

Boy, is the Charlotte Johanssen I baby-sat for today different from the Charlotte I used to sit for last year. She has grown up so much! Skipping a grade was the right thing to do for her. She's bouncy and happy and full of ideas, and she even has a "best friend" -- a girl in her class named Sophie McCann. (Last week her "best friend" was Vanessa Pike. I remember when "best friend" meant almost nothing -- just whoever your current good friend was. Do you guys remember, too?)

Oh, well. I'm way off the subject. Anyway, there's not much to say. Charlotte's easy to sit for. I brought the Kid-Kit over, and we had a great afternoon.

Actually, there *was* more to say, but Stacey couldn't write it in the club notebook because she didn't want me to read it! Something had happened that day that I wasn't going to find out about until my birthday, which was quickly drawing nearer.

Stacey showed up at the Johanssens' after school with her Kid-Kit. A Kid-Kit is something us baby-sitters invented to entertain the kids we sit for. We don't always bring them with us (because the novelty would wear off, as Kristy says), but we bring them along on rainy days or sometimes in between as surprises. A Kid-Kit is a box (we each decorated our own) filled with games and books from our homes, plus coloring books and activity books that we pay for out of the club treasury. Charlotte, especially, likes the Kid-Kits.

When Stacey rang the Johanssens' bell, it was answered by a bouncy Charlotte. "Hi, Stace, hi! Come on in! Oh, you brought the Kid-Kit! Goody!"

Dr. Johanssen appeared behind Charlotte and smiled as Stacey walked through the doorway. "Charlotte's speaking in exclamation points these days," she said fondly.

"Did you have a good day at school, Char?" asked Stacey.

"Yes." (Bounce, bounce, bounce.) "We're learning fractions! And map skills. I love map skills!" (Bounce, bounce.)

"And how are you doing, Stacey?" asked Dr. Johanssen. (Charlotte's mother knows about Stacey's diabetes. She's not her doctor, but she's helped her through some rough times. She's always willing to answer any questions Stacey has.)

"I'm fine, thanks," replied Stacey. "I was getting a little shaky before, but my doctor adjusted my insulin. Now I'm feeling okay again. And I gained a little weight."

"Well, that's a good sign, hon."

"Stacey, is *Paddington Takes the Air* in the Kid-Kit?" Charlotte interrupted.

"Yes," replied Stacey. "And *Tik-Tok of Oz*, too."

Dr. Johanssen smiled at her daughter. "I better get going," she said. "I've got a couple of patients to look in on at the hospital, and some work to do in the children's clinic. Mr. Johanssen will be home around six, Stacey. You know where his office number is. Oh, and if you don't mind, could you put a casserole in the oven at five o'clock? You'll see a blue dish in the refrigerator. Just set the oven to three-fifty, okay?"

"Sure," replied Stacey.

As soon as Dr. Johanssen was out the door, Charlotte took Stacey by the hand, led her into the living room, and pulled her onto the floor. She opened the Kid-Kit eagerly and began pulling things out: a coloring book, a connect-the-dots book, crayons, Magic Markers, drawing paper, Candyland, ("Too babyish," remarked Charlotte), Spill and Spell, a Barbie doll, and at last the Paddington book and the Oz book. Underneath them she found one more book, a Dr. Seuss story called *Happy Birthday to You*.

"Hey, what's this?" asked Charlotte, opening the cover. "I never saw it before."

"I just added it to the Kid-Kit," Stacey told her. "I liked that book a lot when I was younger."

Charlotte glanced at the busy pictures and the funny words. "Let's read this instead," she said.

"Instead of Paddington?" asked Stacey.

"Yes. I like birthdays." Charlotte settled herself in Stacey's lap, even though she's almost too big to do that, and Stacey began to read.

Now, Charlotte is perfectly capable of reading to herself. After all, she skipped a grade. She's incredibly smart, but she loves to be read to. So Stacey read her the long, silly story.

When she was done, Charlotte leaned her head back and sighed. "That's just the way I'd like my birthday to be."

"When is your birthday?" asked Stacey.

"In June. I'll be nine. I can't wait."

"But you've just turned eight."

"I know. But nine sounds like a good age to be. It sounds so grown up."

Stacey smiled. She remembered when she longed to be nine. "It's almost Mary Anne's birthday," she told Charlotte. "She's going to be thirteen."

"Really?" squealed Charlotte, twisting around to look at Stacey.

"Yup."

"Gosh. Thirteen is *old*."

"She'll be a teenager."

"Is she going to have a party?"

"You know, I don't know," said Stacey. "Probably not."

"How come?" asked Charlotte.

Stacey shrugged. "Well, maybe she'll have a little party. Us baby-sitters will go over to her house or something."

"You guys should *give* her a party."

Stacey thought about that. But before she could say anything, Charlotte rushed on, "No, no! Hey, I've got it! You should give her a *surprise* party!"

"Oh, I don't know, Char."

But Charlotte was so excited that she didn't hear Stacey. She stood up and began jumping up down. "Really, Stacey! A surprise party. You invite all of Mary Anne's friends to come at one time, and you invite Mary Anne for half an hour later. Then everybody hides in the dark, and when Mary Anne comes over, you switch the lights on," (Charlotte made a great flourish with her hand), "and everybody jumps out and yells 'surpri-ise'!"

Stacey smiled. "Charlotte, that's a really terrific idea, but Mary Anne is shy. I don't think she'd like to be surprised that way."

"She wouldn't?"

"No. She doesn't like being the center of attention — you know, having everyone look at her."

"Oh." Charlotte sat down again. "How'd she like just a little surprise?"

"What do you mean?"

"Well, maybe you could have a regular party but bring out a surprise cake for Mary Anne."

"You know, that's not a bad idea. I've been wanting to give a party anyway. I don't think Mary Anne would mind a surprise *cake*. After all, we're only doing it because we like her. She should feel flattered."

"Yeah," said Charlotte. "What kind of party

would you tell Mary Anne it was?"

"Just a party, I guess. Back-to-school, or something like that. A chance for all our friends to get together after the summer."

What Stacey didn't tell Charlotte was that she was already thinking about the guest list — and the list included boys.

At home that night, Stacey began to make plans. My birthday was on a Monday, so Stacey asked her parents if she could have a party at her house the Friday before. Her parents gave her their permission. They especially liked the idea of the surprise cake.

Stacey started her guest list: Kristy, Claudia, Dawn, and me (of course), Dori Wallingford, Pete Black, Howie Johnson, Emily Bernstein, Rick Chow. She didn't worry about whether there were an equal number of boys and girls. She was going to tell each person to bring a date! Stacey's party would be one of the first boy/girl parties our class ever had!

The next day, Stacey made other lists:

Food — potato chips and dip, pretzels, Doritos, M&M's, pizzas, soda, a big salad (more for Stacey and Dawn than anyone else) and a large birthday cake to be ordered from the Village Bakery.

Supplies — paper plates, cups, napkins, etc.

To do — start calling guests, check tape collection, buy me a birthday present.

Stacey's plans were elaborate. She told each guest except me that she was giving a party and was going to surprise me with a cake. The guests were supposed to buy a present and keep quiet about the cake. Stacey told me only that she was giving a party. She hinted (not very subtly) that I'd probably want to ask Logan.

I got so caught up in the idea of inviting Logan that it never dawned on me that the party would have something to do with my birthday.

And that, of course, was just what Stacey had been counting on.

CHAPTER 10

The Remember September Dance was on a Friday. Dad had not only given me permission to go with Logan, he'd seemed happy about it. In fact, he'd given me his Bellair's Department Store charge card and told me I could buy a new outfit.

When he handed me the card, his eyes looked sort of teary. I hugged him tight.

A few days later, the entire Baby-sitters Club went to Bellair's to find an outfit for me. We descended on the store after school. Everyone began pulling me in different directions.

"Shoes," said Claudia.

"Juniors," said Dawn.

"Underwear," said Stacey.

"Sportswear," said Kristy.

"*Sportswear!*" the rest of us exclaimed.

Kristy shrugged. "This isn't the prom, you know. You might find a nice sweater in Sportswear. Or an accessory."

"We'll keep it in mind," said Dawn. "Let's go to Juniors first. You can find a dress there, Mary Anne. Then we'll buy shoes to go with it."

"And underwear," said Stacey.

"If necessary," I added.

In the junior department I tried on a green sweater dress that made me look like a mermaid, and a yellow sweater dress that made me look as big as a house. Then Claudia handed me a full white skirt with the words Paris, Rome, and London, and sketchy pink and blue pictures of the Eiffel Tower, the Tower Bridge, and other stuff scrawled all over it. She matched it up with a pink shirt and a baggy pink sweater. I would never, ever have tried on that skirt, but with the shirt and sweater it looked really cool.

In the shoe department we found white slip-ons with pink and blue edging that matched the pink and blue in the skirt. I'd never have looked twice at those shoes, either, but with the rest of the outfit they were perfect.

I charged everything, and talked Stacey out of the underwear department and Kristy out of the sportswear department. I'm not much on shopping, and I'd spent enough of Dad's money already.

* * *

I might have felt calm and cool while we were shopping on Thursday. I was even feeling okay while I did my homework that night. But the next day during school my stomach began to feel queasy, and by that afternoon I was a nervous wreck.

"I must be crazy," I told my friends as school let out. "I'm going to a dance and I don't know *how* to dance. And what if Logan and I can't think of anything to say to each other? What if I stomp on his feet while I'm trying to dance? What if I spill something on him?"

"You know what?" said Kristy. "I say we cancel today's club meeting and go over to Mary Anne's instead. We can pay Janine a couple of dollars to answer the phone for us. Then we can help you get ready for the dance, Mary Anne. I'll walk home with you guys, call Charlie, and tell him where I am so he can pick me up later."

That was just what we did. We gathered in my bedroom. Dawn inspected my outfit and ended up ironing the skirt and shirt for me.

Kristy looked at the soles of my new shoes. "Aughh!" she cried. "Mary Anne, scuff up the bottoms of those or you'll slip at the dance and fall flat on your face."

"Oh, no," I moaned. "Something else to worry about."

Stacey showed me a few easy dance steps.

Claudia gave me some tips on Logan. Things like, "Let him hold doors open for you and get you punch. If he brings you a corsage, wear it no matter what color it is."

"What if it's dead?" asked Kristy, giggling.

Claudia scowled at her.

At 5:30, everyone left. My friends were all going to the dance, too. Kristy and Dawn were going stag, Stacey was going with Howie Johnson, and Claudia was going with Austin Bentley, whom she'd gone out with a few times before. I was glad they would all be there.

My dad volunteered to pick up everyone in the club and take us to the dance. Logan and I had arranged to meet at the entrance to the gym at 7:30. Dad dropped the five of us off at school at precisely 7:25. I leaned over and kissed his cheek. " 'Bye," I said. "Thanks for driving us."

"Have fun, honey."

My friends and I got out of the car with a chorus of "thank you's."

"Remember," I called to Dad as I shut the door, "Mr. McGill will drive us home. The dance is over at nine-thirty."

As I watched the taillights of the car disappear in the parking lot, part of me wished I were with my father, heading to our safe home where I could be alone and not have to worry about people and dancing and spilling punch and slipping in my new shoes. But the rest of me was excited.

I joined my friends and we walked to the gym in a noisy bunch. We were all smoothing our hair and picking lint from our clothes and fussing with our jewelry. I thought we made a pretty good-looking group. Claudia was wearing short, tight-fitting black pants and a big white shirt that said BE-BOP all over it in between pictures of rock and roll dancers. She had fixed a floppy blue bow in her hair. Stacey was wearing a white T-shirt under a hot pink jumpsuit. Dawn and Kristy looked more casual. Dawn was wearing a green and white oversized sweater and stretchy green pants. Kristy was wearing a white turtleneck shirt under a pink sweater with jeans. We just couldn't seem to get her out of blue jeans.

That evening while I was getting dressed, I'd imagined how Logan and I would meet at the door. I'd spot him from across the hallway and walk over to him ever so casually.

"Hi, Logan," I'd say softly.

"Hi, Mary Anne," he'd reply, and he'd hold out a sweet-smelling pink carnation.

As soon as we entered the hall, my dream was shattered. It was a mob scene, wall-to-wall laughing, screaming kids. I stood on my tiptoes and looked all around. After a few seconds I spotted Logan. He was across the hall. Twenty thousand people were between us.

"Logan!" I called. I jumped up and down and waved my hands, but since I'm short, it didn't do any good.

"I see Logan," I told my friends. "I better try to get to him."

"Okay," replied Kristy. "See you later."

"Good luck!" added Dawn excitedly.

I elbowed and squeezed and shoved my way through the kids. When I finally reached Logan, I felt as if I'd just fought a battle. I was hot and sweaty, and the dance hadn't even started.

"Hi — *oof* — hi, Logan," I said as someone slammed into me from behind.

"Hi," replied Logan. Then, "Here," he said ruefully, handing me a smushed orange flower. "Sorry about that. I dropped it and someone stepped on it."

The flower (whatever it was) looked absolutely horrible against my pink sweater, but I pinned it on anyway.

"Thanks," I said.

Logan smiled. "Mah play-sure," he drawled. "Come on. Let's dance."

He led me inside. The only really good thing

I can say about the gymnasium was that it was less crowded than the hallway. I couldn't appreciate the decorations or the refreshments table or the band. I was too busy worrying.

There I was — actually at the dance. In a few minutes, the entire school would see that I had no business being there.

Luckily, Logan wasn't too keen on the idea of dancing until a lot of other people were dancing, so we stood by the food for a long time. We drank three cups of punch each, and ate handfuls of cookies. I couldn't think of a thing to say to Logan. He kept asking me questions, and I kept answering them . . . and then the conversation would lag. I sneaked a peek at my watch. Eight-fifteen.

Finally Logan took my hand. "Want to dance?" he asked.

I nodded. What could I say? No? After all, we were *there* to dance.

By that time, the gym was so crowded that there was barely room to move around. I tried to remember the steps Stacey had shown me. Then I tried to imitate Logan.

Imitating Logan turned out to be fun. He smiled when he realized what I was doing, and began fooling around, dancing sort of the way I imagined King Kong would. I kept up with him. Logan started to laugh. He waved his hands in the air. I waved mine. He stomped his feet and spun in a circle. I stomped my feet and spun in a circle. Logan was laughing hysterically, and I was feeling pretty good myself. He put his arm across my shoulder and kicked his legs Rockette-style. I kicked my legs.

One shoe flew off.

It sailed through the air, narrowly missing Mr. Kingbridge, our vice-principal. It hit a wall and fell to the floor. Mr. Kingbridge picked it up. Leaving a speechless Logan behind, I had to limp through the crowd and claim my shoe.

Please, please, I prayed, let me wake up and find out that this is all a nightmare.

But it wasn't. A whole bunch of kids had seen my flying shoe and they were laughing. By the time I'd put it on and was wending my way back to Logan, he was standing with Stacey and Dawn, and the three of *them* were laughing, too. I had never, never, never been so embarrassed in my whole life. How could I have been feeling so happy just a few moments earlier? I should have known something like this would happen. I am not the kind of person who's cut out for boys or dances or parties. I'm just not. I *knew* this evening was going to be horrible.

"Well, *I* don't think it's so funny," I said stiffly to my friends and marched over to the bleachers which lined one wall of the gym.

"Mary Anne!" Logan called.

But I could hear Dawn say, "Let her go. I think she wants to be alone."

She was right. Except that I wanted to be aloner than by myself in a gym with twenty thousand people. I wanted to be by myself in my room . . . in bed . . . under the covers.

From my perch on the top row of bleachers, I watched Logan dance with Dawn. When the song was over, he climbed the bleachers and sat down next to me. "Mary Anne," he said, "everyone's already forgotten about your shoe. Don't you want to dance?"

I shook my head. Logan brought us some more punch and we drank it while we watched the kids below. After three more songs, Logan said, "Now?"

I shook my head again. "But why don't you go dance?" I didn't really mean it, but I felt I had to say it since Logan looked incredibly bored.

"Are you sure?" he asked.

"Yeah. Go ahead."

So Logan trotted down the bleachers. He danced with Stacey, then Claudia, then Kristy. Then he began with Dawn again. He even broke in on Austin Bentley the next time he wanted to dance with Claudia. In between dances he kept coming back to me, but I couldn't bear to leave the safety of the bleachers. I looked at my watch a million, billion times, waiting for nine-thirty to arrive.

When it did, Logan climbed the bleachers once again. "You'll come down *now*, won't you?" he asked with a little smile.

I smiled back, relieved that he wasn't mad. "Sure," I said.

As we approached the door to the gym I added, "Thank you for the flower."

"Thanks for coming with me. I'm glad you did."

"Honest?"

"Honest. Dancing with you was really fun. No girl has ever fooled around with me like that. Most of them like to prove how well they can dance."

Really? I thought. Well, maybe I could try it again at the next dance. . . . If there was a next dance with Logan.

CHAPTER 11

Friday

Neither Dawn nor I ever want to hear the word "memory" again. Karen, Andrew, and David Michael played that game all evening while Dawn was over to spend the night, and they drove us crazy with their arguing! I was glad Karen wasn't scaring everyone with her stories about Morbidda Destiny and the ghost of Ben Brewer, but — when she's telling her tales, there's no fighting. On the other hand, Mom says she'd rather see Karen and David Michael fight than ignore each other. She says ignoring each other would be a much worse stepfamily problem — at least when they fight they're interacting. But there must be something in between ignoring and fighting..... oh yeah — scaring each other.

Kristy's notebook entry was complete in terms of baby-sitting concerns, but not in terms of everything that happened that night. A lot of talking (especially about my birthday) went on, but I didn't find out about it until much later.

Let me start at the beginning, though. It was Friday night again. Logan hadn't seemed too upset about the dance. In fact, he'd called me the next morning to ask if I wanted to go over to school to watch the junior varsity football game. On Monday and Tuesday he'd sat with our club at lunchtime. On Wednesday, he and I had sat by ourselves (but we joined the club again the next day). On Thursday he had invited me to go to the movies on Friday.

Needless to say, I was ecstatic! We still had a little trouble talking sometimes, but Logan always seemed so *interested* in me, and in everything I did or said. It's hard to be shy around someone who thinks you're wonderful.

On Friday night, Kristy was stuck at home baby-sitting for Karen, Andrew, and David Michael, so her mother and Watson said she could invite a friend over. Usually she would have invited me, but since I was busy with Logan, she asked Dawn to come over.

Talk about ecstatic. Dawn still hasn't gotten over the days when Kristy was jealous of Dawn's friendship with me, and would barely speak to her. And Kristy had never invited just Dawn to sleep over. So Dawn gladly accepted. Her mother drove her to the Brewer mansion not long after Kristy's mom and Watson had left.

When Dawn rang the doorbell, she heard shrieks coming from inside, only they sounded like terrified shrieks, not joyful ones.

Nervously, Dawn turned around and looked at her mother who was waiting in the car until Dawn was safely inside. What should she do? She didn't want to call her mother to the door and then find out there was nothing wrong. That would be embarrassing.

Dawn rang the bell again. More shrieking. She screwed up her courage. With a shaking hand, she turned the knob and slowly peered around the door and into the front hall.

"Aughh! Aughh! Au — Dawn?"

"Karen?"

"Oh, I thought you were Morbidda Destiny, creeping into our house to put a sp — "

"Karen, that is enough." It was Kristy's impatient voice. "I don't want to hear another word about poor old Mrs. Porter — or the ghost of Ben Brewer — tonight. And I mean it." Kristy appeared in the hall, followed by Louie the collie, and Dawn waved to her mother who waved back, then started down the drive.

"Okay, okay." Karen flounced off.

"Sorry about that," said Kristy. She reached out to help Dawn with her things. "I was in the kitchen. I could hear Karen screaming and I knew what she was doing, but I was too far away to stop her."

Dawn grinned. "That's okay." She held her hand out to Louie, who gave it a halfhearted lick.

"I don't think Louie's in top condition tonight," said Kristy. "He's getting old. Well, come on. We'll put your things upstairs. Then we'll have to keep an eye on the kids. After all, I'm baby-sitting."

"No problem. You know I like the kids."

Kristy and Dawn settled Andrew, Karen, and David Michael on the living room floor with the Memory set. Louie lay down nearby, his head resting mournfully on his paws. Then Kristy and Dawn retreated to a couch, where they sprawled out with a box of graham crackers — one of the few snack foods they'll both eat, since Kristy considers graham crackers semi-junk food and Dawn considers them semi-health food.

"I wonder what Mary Anne and Logan are doing right now," said Kristy.

Dawn looked at her watch. "The movie's probably just beginning."

"Yeah. The theater's all dark. . . ."

"Maybe they're holding hands. . . ."

"Kristy!" shouted Karen. "David Michael cheated. He just peeked at one of the cards." Karen stood indignantly over the blue cards that were arranged facedown on the floor.

(I guess I should explain here how Memory is played. It's very simple. The game consists of a big stack of cards. On each is a picture — and each card has one, and only one, matching card. The cards are laid out facedown. The players take turns turning two cards over. If someone gets a pair, he or she goes again. When all the cards have been matched up, the winner is the one with the most pairs. Simple, right?)

Wrong!

"I did not cheat!" cried David Michael. "It's a rule. Each player gets one peeksie during a game."

"Show me where it says anything about a peeksie in the rules," answered Kristy, holding her hand out.

"Well, that's how we play at Linny's."

"Why don't you play by the rulebook?" suggested Kristy.

The game continued.

"Where were we?" Kristy asked Dawn. "Oh, yeah. In the dark theater."

"Holding hands — maybe," said Dawn. "I wonder if they'll, you know, kiss."

"Ew!" exclaimed Kristy, looking disgusted, but then she grew quiet. "You know," she said after several moments, "maybe they will. Mary Anne seems more serious about Logan than Claudia ever was about Trevor."

"How do you mean?"

"Well, she's not silly about him. Remember how Claudia used to giggle about Trevor all the time? It was as if she liked the idea of going out with him better than she liked Trevor himself."

"Karen! No fair! You didn't let me finish my turn!" Now Andrew was shrieking.

"Woof?" asked Louie from his spot on the floor.

"Hey, hey!" cried Kristy.

"I got a match and Karen took her turn anyway! No fair! No fair!"

"Andrew, I just for*got*, okay? Finish your turn," said Karen.

"But you've already turned over two cards," said David Michael indignantly. "And Andrew saw them. He knows where two more cards are. So nothing's fair now. The game's ruined."

"Excuse me," said Kristy, "but did you *all* see which cards Karen turned over?"

"Yes," chorused the three kids.

"Then *every*thing's fair. You all got an advantage. Think of it as a bonus or something. Andrew, finish your turn."

Kristy sighed. "You know," she said, picking at a tiny piece of lint on her sweater, "I was always the brave one and Mary Anne was always the scaredy-cat. Now everything's reversed. And suddenly she's . . . I don't know . . . ahead of me, and I've been left behind."

Dawn nodded. "But you're still her friend, one of her very best friends."

"I know. I just have a feeling this is going to be an awful year. I moved away from you guys, and Mary Anne's moving away from me, if you know what I mean. And I haven't made any friends here in Watson's neighborhood. My brothers have, but I haven't." Kristy stretched her hand toward Louie, but he wouldn't come over to her for a pat. He looked exhausted.

"It might help," said Dawn carefully, "if you stopped thinking of it as Watson's neighborhood and started thinking of it as your own."

"Karen, you give those back!" This time, the indignant voice belonged to David Michael. "Kristy, she keeps hiding my pairs under the couch. Look!" David Michael pulled up the slipcover on the loveseat he and Karen were leaning against. He revealed a row of paired Memory cards.

"They're not his, they're mine!" squawked Karen.

"Are not!"

"Are, too!"

Kristy stood up. "The game is over," she whispered.

Karen and David Michael had to stop screaming in order to hear her.

"What?" they said.

"The game is over."

Kristy's patience had worn thin, although she kept her temper. A half an hour later, the three children were in bed, and Dawn and Kristy were seated side by side on Kristy's big bed. Louie was sacked out at the end. The portable color TV that Watson had given Kristy was on, but neither Dawn nor Kristy was paying attention.

"Clothes?" Dawn was saying.

"Tapes, maybe," Kristy suggested. They were trying to decide what to get me for my birthday.

"It has to be something she wants, but that she won't be embarrassed to open in front of boys."

"I really wish Stacey hadn't decided on a boy/girl party," said Kristy woefully.

"How come?" asked Dawn.

"Well, who are *you* going to invite?"

Dawn's eyes widened. "Gosh, I hadn't thought about it."

"Even if I could think of a boy I wanted to go with, I wouldn't know how to ask him," confessed Kristy.

"You know who I like?" Dawn said conspiratorially.

"Who?"

"Bruce Schermerhorn. He's in my math class. You know him?"

"I think so."

"He's really cute."

"I *could* ask Alan Gray," said Kristy. "He's a pest, but we always end up doing stuff together. At least I'd know what to expect from him . . . I think."

Kristy and Dawn looked at each other, sighed, and leaned back against their pillows. Louie sighed, too. Eighth grade came complete with problems nobody had counted on.

CHAPTER 12

*R*ing, ring, ring.

"Hello?"

"Hi, Mary Anne."

"Logan! Hi." (I was always surprised to hear his voice on the phone.)

"How're you doing?"

"Fine. How are you?" (It was four o'clock on a weekday afternoon. We'd just seen each other an hour earlier.)

"Fine. Guess what's on TV tonight."

"What?"

"*Meatballs*. Have you ever seen it? It's really funny."

"I don't think so. I mean, I don't think I've seen it."

"It's on at eight. Try to watch it."

"I will."

"So? What's going on?"

"I'm going to baby-sit for Jackie Rodowsky tomorrow. The last time I sat for him, he fell out of a tree, fell down the front steps, and fell off the bed. But he didn't get hurt at all."

Logan laughed. "That kid should wear a crash helmet," he joked.

"And carry a first-aid kit," I added.

There was a pause. I had no idea how to fill the silence. Why did this always happen with Logan? There were hardly any pauses when I talked to the members of the Baby-sitters Club. I knew I was blushing and was glad Logan couldn't see me.

"Want me to tell you about *Meatballs*?" asked Logan.

"Sure," I replied, relieved. A movie plot could take awhile to explain.

And Logan took awhile. In fact, he took so long that we reached my phone conversation limit. My dad still has a few rules that he's strict about, and one of them is that no phone conversation can last longer than ten minutes. Even though Dad was at work, I felt I had to obey the rule. For one thing, what if he'd been trying to call me for the last ten minutes?

Logan reached a stopping place, and I knew I had to interrupt him.

"Um, Logan?" I said.

"Yeah?"

"I hate to say this, but — "

"Your time's up?" he finished for me.

"Yeah. Sorry."

"That's okay. So are you going to watch *Meatballs*?"

"I'll try. If I get my homework done."

"Great. Well . . . see you tomorrow."

"See you tomorrow."

We hung up.

Whewwwww. I let out a long, slow breath. I love talking to Logan, but it makes me nervous.

Ring, ring.

Aughh! Dad *had* been trying to call! And I'd been on the phone for over twelve minutes.

"Hello?" I said guiltily. Excuses began flying around in my head: I'd needed a homework assignment explained. Someone else had needed homework explained. The phone had accidentally fallen off the hook.

"Hi, Mary Anne!" said a cheerful voice.

"Oh, Stacey. It's only you!" I exclaimed.

"*Only* me! Thanks a lot."

"No, you don't understand. I thought you were Dad. I mean, I thought you were going to be Dad. See, I've been on the phone for — Oh, never mind."

"More than ten minutes?" asked Stacey, giggling.

"Yeah."

"Well, listen. I just wanted to make sure

you were coming to my party — and that you'd invited Logan."

"Well . . ." The thing is, I'd been putting that party off a little. I was nervous about asking my father if I could go to a boy/girl party, and even more nervous about inviting Logan. How do you go about inviting a boy to a party?

"Mary Anne?"

"What?"

"Are you coming and have you invited Logan?" she repeated.

"I don't know, and, no, I haven't."

"Mary *A*-anne."

"Okay, okay. Sorry. Really I am." (I didn't know then why Stacey sounded so exasperated. I was the guest of honor at her party, but I had no idea.)

"Get off the phone and call Logan."

"I, um, have to call my father, too. I have to get permission to go to the party first."

"So call him, *then* call Logan."

"I've been on the phone since four."

"The rule is ten minutes per call. Just keep these calls short. It's the easiest rule in the world to get around. My mother put a five-minute limit on my calls to Laine Cummings in New York. So I just keep calling her back. If I call six times we can talk for half an hour."

I laughed. "All right. I'll call Dad."

"Call me back after you've talked to Logan."

"Okay. 'Bye."

I depressed the button on the phone, listened for the dial tone, and called my father at his office.

His secretary put me through right away.

"Hi, Dad," I said.

"Oh, hi, Mary Anne. I'm in the middle of something. Is this important?"

I was forced to talk fast. "Sort of," I replied. "Stacey's having a party at her house. It's for both boys and girls. We're supposed to ask guests. Can I go? And can I invite Logan?"

"Will Mr. and Mrs. McGill be at home during the party?"

"Yes," I said, even though I hadn't asked Stacey about that. I was sure they would be at home, though.

"What time is the party?"

"It starts at six."

"You may go if you'll be home by ten, and if you *meet* Logan *at* the party."

"Oh, thanks, Dad, thanks! I promise I'll be home by ten! I promise everything!"

I called Logan with a bit more enthusiasm than I'd felt before. I punched his phone number jauntily — K-L-five-one-zero-one-eight.

Logan answered right away.

"Hi," I said. "It's me again. Mary Anne Spier."

"I know your voice!" he exclaimed.

"Oh, sorry."

"Don't apologize."

The call was already going badly. I wished I could rewind time and start over.

"Um . . ." I began.

"Hey," said Logan, more softly. "I'm really glad you called. You never call me. I always call you. I'm glad you felt, you know, comfortable enough to call."

(This was better, but still not the conversation I'd imagined.) "Well, I have to ask you something. Not a favor. I mean . . . Stacey's having a party. I wanted to know if you'd — you'd go with me. If you don't want to, that's okay," I rushed ahead. "I'll understand."

"Slow down, Mary Anne! Of course I want to go. When is it?"

I gave him the details.

"Great," he said. "I can't wait."

As long as I was doing so well, I decided to ask Logan one more question. "Have you thought anymore about joining the Baby-sitters Club?"

Pause. "Well, I said I didn't want to join."

"I know, but . . ."

"I'll think about it some more, okay?"

"Okay." (After all, the rest of us hadn't decided that we *wanted* Logan to join.)

There was some muffled whispering at Logan's end of the phone, and then he said, sounding highly annoyed, "Mary Anne, I have to get off the phone. I'm really sorry. My little sister has a call to make that she thinks is more important than this."

"It is!" cried a shrill voice.

I laughed. "I better get off, too," I told Logan.

So we hung up. But I had one more call to make. "Hi, Stacey?"

"Hi!" she said. "Did you call Logan already? Did you call your dad?"

"Yes and yes."

"And?"

"And I can come and Logan's coming, too."

"Oh, great! Awesome! Fabulous! I can't believe it!"

Stacey was so excited that her excitement was contagious. My heart began pounding, and I was grinning.

We hung up.

Ring, ring.

"Hello?"

"Mary Anne! What on earth have you been doing? What happened to your ten-minute limit? I've been calling you forever!"

"Kristy?"

"You ought to get call-waiting or something. Did your dad take away your limit? . . . Oh, yeah, this is Kristy." *(Click, click.)* "Oh, hold on, Mary Anne. We've got another call coming in over here." (Kristy put me on hold for a few seconds.) "Mary Anne?" she said, when she was back on. "That was Stacey. I better talk to her. Call you later. 'Bye!"

The plans for the birthday surprise were in full swing — and I suspected nothing.

CHAPTER 13

I dressed carefully for Stacey's party, even though I didn't have much choice about what to wear. My best-looking outfit was the one I'd worn to the dance, so I decided to put it on again.

By six o'clock I was ready and had to kill time. Stacey had originally said that the party would start at six, but that afternoon she'd called to say that everything was going wrong and could I come at six-thirty instead?

"Sure," I'd replied. "I'll call Logan and let him know."

"Oh, no. Don't bother," said Stacey quickly. "I'll call him. I have to call everyone else." She was talking very fast. I decided she must be nervous about the party.

So at 6:15 that night, dressed in my famous-cities skirt, the pink sweater, and the lethal white shoes, I was standing around in the kitchen while my father started his dinner. At 6:25, I flicked on the TV and watched the news. At 6:35, I decided not to leave quite yet because I didn't want to be the first to arrive at the party. Finally, at 6:40, I left for Stacey's. I wished I could have walked with Claudia, but she had told me that she and her mom were going to pick up Austin Bentley first. I kind of got the feeling that I wasn't wanted.

When I rang Stacey's bell at 6:45 I could hear an awful lot of voices inside. Stacey flung the door open. "Oh, you're here!" she cried. "Come on in!"

I stepped inside.

"Let's go downstairs. Everyone's in the rec room," she said giddily.

"Gosh," I replied, "it sounds like everyone else has already arrived." I glanced at my watch. "I'm sorry I'm so late."

"Oh, you're not — not late," said Stacey. "I guess the others were early."

All of them? I wondered. "Is Logan here?" I asked.

"Yup. You're the last to arrive."

That made me feel a little uncomfortable, but I tried to shrug the feeling off. I still wasn't suspicious. After all, I was used to feeling uncomfortable in a crowd.

Stacey and I descended the stairs to the rec

room. On the way down, I thought of something important. "Stacey, your parents are home, aren't they?"

"Yes," Stacey answered, "but I made them promise not to come into the rec room. I think they're in the kitchen. That way, they can keep an eye on the food and an ear on the party."

From my vantage point halfway up the stairs, the start of Stacey's party looked a lot like the start of the school dance. Although the tape deck was playing loudly, no one was dancing. The girls were bunched up in a corner, and the boys were bunched up by the table where Stacey had put out pretzels, potato chips, M&M's, soda, and salad.

Austin Bentley was tossing pretzels in the air and trying to catch them in his mouth. Mostly, he missed.

Alan Gray had put yellow M&M's in his eyes and was going around telling the boys he was Little Orphan Annie.

Pete Black was dunking potato chips in his Coke before eating them.

Across the room, Dori Wallingford was showing her new bracelet to Claudia, who was pretending to be impressed, but who was really watching Austin toss the pretzels in his mouth.

Kristy was whispering to Dawn, who was giggling.

114

Emily Bernstein was saying loudly, "Alan Gray is *so* immature," and glaring at Kristy — for having invited him, I guess.

As Stacey led me down the stairs it seemed — for just an instant — that everyone stopped talking, that the entire room paused. But I decided it was my imagination. The room was as noisy as ever when I reached the bottom of the steps.

I looked for Logan. Before I found him, I felt a hand on my shoulder. I turned around and there he was.

"Hey," he said, giving me his wide, warm grin. "How ya doin'?"

"Great," I replied.

"Boy, you look nice."

"Thanks, but this is the same outfit I wore to the dance."

"You still look nice."

A phone on the wall nearby began to ring. "Mary Anne, can you get that?" yelled Stacey from across the room.

I picked up the receiver. "Hello, McGills' residence."

With all the music and talking, it was hard to hear the person on the other end of the line, but I *thought* the voice said, "Hello, this is the Atlanta Pig Corporation. When would you like your pig farm delivered?"

115

"What?" I shouted.

"We have a pig farm reserved in the name of Stacey McGill. When would you like us to ship it to you?"

"Just a sec." I paused, putting my hand over the mouthpiece. "Stacey!" I yelled. "Come here!"

Stacey edged through the rec room. "What?"

"It's for you. Something about . . . a pig farm?"

Stacey got on the phone, frowning. "Hello . . . A *pig* farm? . . . Justin Forbes, is that you? You are *so* immature!" *Clunk.* She hung up. Stacey turned to Logan and me. "Justin's all bent out of shape because he wasn't invited to the party," she informed us. She went back to Claudia and the other girls.

Immediately, the phone began to ring again.

"*I'll* get it this time," said Logan, reaching for the receiver. "Hello, Disneyland. Goofy speaking. How may I help you?"

I giggled.

"He hung up," said Logan, pretending to look surprised. "I can't imagine why."

Nobody was dancing and only the boys were eating. Logan steered me toward a couch. "Let's sit down," he said. "Wait, I'll be right back."

I sat, and a few minutes later, Logan returned with two cups of soda and a bag of pretzels. We sipped our sodas in silence for a few moments but for the first time, our silence seemed comfortable, not uncomfortable. Then Logan asked me a question and we began to talk. We talked about school and our families. Logan told me about Louisville, and I told him about wanting a cat. We talked for so long I lost track of the time. I didn't even hear all the noise around me, except for when Alan Gray shouted, "Let's play Spin the Bottle!" and Emily Bernstein shouted back, "You are *so* immature, Alan!"

It was as if Logan and I were in our own world, and nobody and nothing else existed. A scary thought occurred to me. Was this part of being in love? Nah. I was only twelve-going-on-thirteen. I couldn't really be in love . . . could I?

"You know," said Logan, polishing off his Pepsi, "I'm glad to be getting to know the real Mary Anne. This *is* the real Mary Anne, isn't it?"

"What do you mean?"

"Well, when I first met you, I liked you okay, but you were so quiet and shy. I've never known anyone as shy as you."

"Believe it or not, I'm better than I used to be."

"You're kidding!"

"No, really. . . . Well, maybe I'm still not very good around boys."

"Yeah?"

"Yeah."

Logan considered that. "If you could just open up more — I mean, be the way you are right now — people would have a much easier time getting to know you. I almost didn't ask you to the dance, you know."

"Why *did* you ask me?"

"Because you're different from other girls. More . . . something."

"More what?" I asked, puzzled. I really wanted to know.

"More serious. Not serious like some old professor, but serious about people. You listen to them and understand them and take them seriously. People like to be taken seriously. It makes them feel worthwhile. But you have a sense of humor, too, which is nice. The only thing is, sometimes you're too sensitive. I really wasn't sure things would work out between us."

"I've always been too sensitive," I told him.

"AUGHH! AUGHH! HELP!"

The room was slowly darkening and everyone was screaming.

"Oh, would you guys grow up," said Stacey's impatient voice as the lights brightened

118

again. "I was dimming the lights. I just wanted to make things more romantic."

I smiled at Logan and we looked around. While we'd been talking, the boys and girls had started to mingle. Claudia and Austin and some other kids were dancing. Alan was torturing Emily with his Little Orphan Annie eyes. Most of the food was gone.

"I'm sending Dad out for pizza now," Stacey informed me.

Mr. McGill returned later with three pizzas (which he wasn't allowed to bring into the rec room) and they were eaten in no time. After Logan and I finished our slices, we sat on the couch again.

For the second time that night, the lights began to dim. Only this time, they went all the way out and nobody screamed. In the darkness, I heard only some muffled whispering and sensed that someone was coming down the steps.

Suddenly the lights were turned on full force, and everyone began singing "Happy Birthday."

I felt totally confused. What was happening? Stacey hadn't said this was a birthday party. Not until the kids sang, "Happy birthday, dear Mary Anne," did I understand. Then I saw that Stacey was at the bottom of the stairs carrying a big birthday cake that said HAPPY BIRTHDAY, MARY ANNE in pink frosting and glittered with lighted candles. Behind her were Kristy and Dawn, each holding a stack of gifts.

Stacey set the cake on a table next to Logan and me. Kristy and Dawn piled the presents on the floor near my feet. Logan held out a small box wrapped in silver paper and tied with a silver bow.

Silence had fallen over the rec room. The song was finished. Austin had paused in his pretzel-throwing. Alan was staring at me with his blind M&M eyes. Pete had stopped in the middle of a dunk, and the soggy potato chip had fallen into his Coke. Claudia, Dori, and Emily were standing in an expectant bunch, a safe distance from Alan, their eyes on me. All the guests were waiting for me to react, to blow out the candles, to cry, or *some*thing.

It was a nightmare. It was like one of those dreams in which you go to school naked, or study and study for an important test and then sleep through your alarm clock and miss it.

I had only one thought: I had to get out of there.

So I did.

I ran up the stairs, out the McGills' front door, and all the way home, leaving my nightmare behind.

CHAPTER 14

"Mary Anne," my father exclaimed as I barged into our house. "What are you doing home so early? I thought you were going to call me for a ride when the party was over."

"Sorry," I replied. I slowed down and caught my breath. I didn't want my father to know anything was wrong. I just couldn't explain this to him.

"Everything okay?" asked Dad.

"Oh, sure. The, um, party broke up early."

Dad looked suspicious. "Were Mr. and Mrs. McGill there?" he asked.

"Oh, yes. Stacey wouldn't let them go into the rec room, but they were right in the kitchen the whole time. Honest. It just wasn't a very good party. No one was having fun. So it kind of ended."

"I'm sorry," said Dad, and he really did look sorry.

"Me, too," I replied. "Well, I'm tired. I guess I'll go to bed."

I went slowly up to my room and stretched out on my bed, but I had no intention of going to sleep. I hadn't even taken my party clothes off. How dare Stacey have done that to me? I thought. She knows how I feel about parties and people and surprises and being the center of attention. My other friends know, too. Especially Kristy and Dawn and Logan. But they had all let it happen.

I was beginning to put the pieces of the puzzle together. Everyone had known about the cake except me. I must have been the only one who was told to arrive at six-thirty. The others had probably come at six, as originally planned, so I wouldn't see them arrive with gifts. That's why Claudia hadn't wanted to go to the party with me.

I lay there, and the memory of the lights coming on flooded back: everyone singing, Stacey with the cake, Kristy and Dawn with the presents. I recalled that Logan had been grinning at me like a Halloween mask. How *could* he? Hadn't we just been talking about how I was shy and quiet? I took people seriously, but no one took *me* seriously.

I felt tears streaming down my cheeks, but I didn't bother to dry them. I had run away.

I had humiliated myself. As mad as I was at Stacey and my friends, I realized that they had wanted to do something nice for me, and I hadn't let them. I'd spoiled everything.

But still . . . how *could* they?

I looked at my watch. I'd only left the party fifteen minutes earlier. Any moment now, Logan or Stacey would call. The thought cheered me. They would apologize for embarrassing me, and invite me back, and say they didn't know what they could have been thinking.

I tiptoed to my door and set it ajar so I'd be sure to hear the phone when it rang. Then I lay on my bed again.

When another ten minutes had gone by, I realized that Stacey (or Logan) was probably going to come over instead, to give things the personal touch. Of course. That was just like them.

I opened my window a crack so I'd hear them when they got to the front door. I hoped Dad had left the porch light on. I peeked outside. He had.

When an hour had gone by and my room was chilly with the night air, I knew that no one was going to call or come over. My stomach felt like I'd swallowed a brick. I'd really blown it this time. I should have seen it coming. My friends had finally had enough of my behavior. I'd gone one step too far. No one likes a party-spoiler, no matter how well he tries to understand that person. And Logan had surely decided that I wasn't right for him after all. I really was just plain too shy.

Well, I was sorry I was different. I couldn't help it. But it was their fault for doing something they knew I wouldn't enjoy.

My anger was no comfort, though. All I could think was that I'd lost my friends. I tried to cheer myself with the thought that the last time that had happened I'd been forced to make a new friend — and I'd found Dawn. But the thought wasn't all that cheery. I didn't want any new friends now. I only wanted Kristy and Dawn and Stacey and Claudia and Logan.

Tomorrow might be a good time to ask my dad for a cat.

I fell asleep with my clothes on and awoke to a beautiful Saturday morning. But it felt bleak to me. As soon as I saw my famous-cities skirt, the awful evening rushed back. I realized that the brick was still in my stomach.

It was nine o'clock. Dad had let me sleep late. I felt as if I hadn't slept at all, though. I staggered to my feet, washed up, and changed my clothes. I found my father in the living room, drinking coffee and reading some papers for work.

"Morning," he greeted me.

"Can we get a cat?" I replied.

Dad raised an eyebrow. "What brought this on? . . . Oh, your birthday, right? I didn't forget, Mary Anne. We'll do something special on the big day. I was thinking of dinner at a restaurant in Stamford. Wouldn't that be fun? I've got some presents, too." Dad grinned. "And I had a little help picking them out, so I know you'll like them."

"That sounds great," I said, mustering a tiny smile, "but this doesn't have anything to do with my birthday. I just want a cat to keep me company. Then I wouldn't feel alone when you're not here."

"I don't know, Mary Anne. We've never had a pet before. We'd need a litter box and a carrier. And what would we do with the cat if we went on vacation?"

"Get Mallory Pike to come feed it?" I suggested.

"Well," said my father, "I'll think about it. Do you know any vets? We'd need a vet, too."

"The Thomases go to Dr. Smith," I told him. "They really like her."

Dad sipped his coffee and stared into space. At last he said, "Okay, I've thought about it. You may get a cat."

All I could say was, "What?" I couldn't believe he'd made the decision so fast.

"You may get a cat," Dad repeated. "If you'll use some of your baby-sitting earnings to buy dishes and toys and a litter box, I'll buy the carrier and pay for food and the vet bills. Consider it an early birthday present. After all, thirteen is an important birthday."

"Oh, Dad! Thanks!" I flung myself at my father, giving him a fierce hug.

"We probably should have gotten a pet a long time ago," he said. "The only two things I ask are that *you* take care of the cat as much as possible — "

"Oh, I will, I will!"

"And that you get the cat, or a kitten, from the animal shelter. Give a home to a pet that really needs one. Most of the animals in the pet store will eventually be sold, but the animals in the shelter are in a bit of trouble."

"No problem," I said. "I'd rather get a stray, too."

Suddenly I had an excuse to do something I'd sort of been thinking about ever since I woke up. I went into the kitchen, closed both doors, and called the Brunos' house.

Logan's little sister answered, shouted, "Logan, it's for you — a gi-irl!" and giggled nonstop until Logan got on the phone.

"Hello?" he said.

I cleared my throat. "Hi, it's me."

"Mary Anne?"

"I thought you always knew my voice," I teased him.

"I didn't expect to hear from you, that's all. I thought you were mad at me."

"You did?"

"Well, actually, we *all* thought you were mad at *us*. I'm really glad you called." Logan sounded relieved.

I bit my lip. "Is that why no one called me last night?" I asked.

"Well . . . yeah. We were sure you never wanted to speak to us again. We're really sorry about what we did. We should have known better."

"Wow," I said. "I thought all of *you* were mad at *me* — for being so, you know, ungrateful. And spoiling the party."

"Oh, boy," said Logan, letting out his breath. "Sorry."

"Me, too. . . . But listen. I have some good news. Dad said I could get a cat! Want to meet me at the animal shelter and help me pick one out?"

"Sure! When? Today?"

"This afternoon. Dad and I have to buy a few things first."

So that morning my father and I went shopping for cat stuff, and that afternoon, we met Logan at the Stoneybrook Animal Shelter. Dad waited in the car so Logan and I could go looking alone.

The shelter was clean and the people were nice, but I sure wouldn't have wanted to be an animal stuck there. It was like an orphanage for pets. Row after row of wire cages, each holding a lost or homeless dog or cat. Most of them looked frightened and nervous.

A woman led Logan and me into the cat area.

"I think I'd like a kitten," I told her.

"Well," she said, "I'm afraid it's the wrong time of year for kittens, so we don't have many. Just one litter. They're over here. Someone left these four kitties outside the shelter a couple of weeks ago without their mother. We weren't sure they were going to make it. But now they're all healthy and frisky."

I peered inside a cage that was larger than most others. The four kittens were snoozing in a relaxed heap on an old blanket. There were two red tabbies, one splotchy, patchy calico, and a gray tiger cat.

"Are they old enough to be separated?" I asked.

The woman nodded.

"Then I want the gray one, please," I said.

Logan nudged me. "Don't you want to play with them first or something? Maybe you'd like one of the others better."

"Nope," I said. "I've always wanted a gray tiger cat, and I've always wanted to name it Tigger after the tiger in *Winnie-the-Pooh*."

This seemed to make sense to Logan.

The woman opened the cage, gently pulled the sleeping kitten from its litter mates, and handed it to me. "It's a boy," she said.

Dad and Logan and I took Tigger home in his carrier, and he cried all the way. He didn't seem to want milk or kitten chow or anything, and refused to leave the carrier, so Logan and I left him in it and watched him fall asleep.

When Tigger was as limp as a little rag doll, Logan reached into his pocket, pulled something out, and handed it to me. It was the silver-wrapped box he'd had at Stacey's party.

"Happy birthday," he said. "I wasn't sure I'd ever be giving this to you. After last night, I thought we were through. I really didn't think things could work out between us. But you took the first step and called me today. I know that wasn't easy. Anyway, happy birthday."

While Tigger napped, I opened the box and found a delicate silver bracelet.

"Oh, thank you," I breathed.

"You're welcome," Logan said softly. "Want to come to the Fifties Fling with me next month?"

Did he have to ask? Of course I did!

CHAPTER 15

Saturday had turned out to be a pretty good day after all, what with Tigger, Logan's birthday present, and Logan's invitation to the dance. But I wasn't through with my apologies. I knew I had to call Stacey, too. So, late in the afternoon, with a now frisky Tigger playing in my lap, I picked up the phone and dialed her number.

"Stacey," I said, a lump rising in my throat, "it's me, Mary Anne."

"Oh."

I couldn't read that "oh" at all. Had it sounded surprised? Annoyed? Sarcastic? But before I could decide what to say next, Stacey mumbled, "I guess you're wondering why I haven't called."

"Well," I replied, "I thought *you* might be wondering why *I* hadn't called."

Then Stacey and I proceeded to have the same sort of conversation that Logan and I had had that morning. Each thought the other was mad, we both apologized, and then we cried a little. I promised to try to be more outgoing (after all, the kids at the party had been my friends), and Stacey promised to try to be more understanding.

"Ow!" I cried as she was finishing her promise.

"What? What?"

"Something bit me!" (Tigger, of course, with his baby teeth, which were like needles.)

I told Stacey all about Tigger then, and she suggested that we hold a special meeting of the Baby-sitters Club at my house the next day so everybody could see him.

It turned out, though, that she had another reason for wanting to hold a meeting at my house, but I didn't find that out until Sunday.

On Sunday afternoon at three o'clock, the doorbell rang.

"Time for our meeting," I told Tigger. I picked him up and carried him to the door so he could meet the first club member.

When I opened the door, though, I found the entire club on our doorstep, along with the remains of my birthday party — a chunk of cake, and all the presents.

"Surprise," whispered Kristy, Dawn, Claudia, and Stacey.

I giggled. "Come on in."

Tigger watched my friends with wide, bright eyes as they settled themselves in the living room. Dad stuck his head in the room, said hello to everybody, and then sensibly retreated to the den.

"You sort of missed the birthday part of your party," Stacey explained, "so we decided to bring it over. You can open your presents, and we'll meet Tigger."

"There are so many presents!" I exclaimed.

"Everyone at the party brought one. And they all wanted you to have them, even after you'd left. So here they are."

"Wow," I said. "Well, you can play with Tigger while I open them."

But Tigger didn't want to play with my friends. The wrapping paper was much more interesting. He rolled on his back, leaped in the air, and batted at the ribbon with his paws.

"He sure is lively," said Claudia.

"I know. We have to have the vet look him over, though. I mean, since he was a stray and all. The shelter gave us this little book on cat care and it said that kittens should be checked for worms and mites. Plus, the vet has to tell us when he's old enough to get his shots."

"Are you going to take him to Dr. Smith?" asked Kristy.

"Yes, I think so. Oh!" I had just opened Dawn's present. It was a blue shirt that matched my famous-cities skirt. "Thank you! This is perfect!" I cried.

I kept on opening. I'd never seen so many presents. Kristy gave me a Smash tape. (They're our favorite group.) Stacey gave me a pair of famous-cities socks. (They were really wild.) And Claudia gave me some jewelry she'd made in her pottery class. "I can't believe you *made* this," I said. "It looks professional."

Most of the other gifts, especially the ones from the boys, were silly. Alan Gray gave me a wind-up dinosaur that shot sparks out of its mouth, and Austin gave me a pin shaped like a cow. When I'd opened everything, Stacey said, "Well, let's kill the cake. You haven't even tasted your own birthday cake, Mary Anne."

I always feel bad eating sweets in front of Stacey, but she doesn't seem to mind. So I divided the cake into four small pieces and Kristy, Claudia, Dawn, and I ate every last crumb, while Stacey polished off a couple of rice cakes. (Yuck.)

"Maybe we'll turn you into a junk-food addict yet," Claudia said to Dawn.

"I don't think so." Dawn made a face. "Now that I've eaten all that sugar, the only thing I want to do is brush my teeth." She settled for rinsing her mouth out.

"You know what?" I said to the members of the Baby-sitters Club. "I think this has been one of my best birthdays ever — and it's not even my birthday yet!"

"Mew," announced Tigger. He was sitting up perfectly straight with his tail wrapped around his front feet, gazing at me with round eyes.

"And you," I said, picking Tigger up gently, "are part of what made my birthday so great."

Tigger looked at me for another moment and then yawned.

Everybody laughed.

"Come to order. Please come to order!" said Kristy. She was wearing a visor and she adjusted it on her head as she settled into Claudia's director's chair.

It was the next afternoon (my birthday), time for a real club meeting. Before she could say another word, the phone rang.

"Hello, Baby-sitters Club," said Stacey.

I listened as Stacey asked questions, and could tell she was talking to Mrs. Pike. We fixed the Pikes up with a sitter, and the phone rang again immediately. It turned out to be one of those days.

After we lined up a sitter for Jenny Prezzioso, Mrs. Barrett called. Then Kristy's mom, Mr. Newton, and Mrs. Rodowsky. By the time we hung up with Jackie's mother, our heads were spinning.

"Oh," groaned Kristy, and the phone rang again.

This time I answered it. "Hello, Baby-sitters Club."

"Hello, my name is Mr. Morgan. I live across the street from Mariel Rodowsky. She recommended your group to me. I need a sitter on Saturday night."

"How many children do you have?" I asked.

"Four. All boys."

"And how old are they?"

Mr. Morgan gave me all the information, and I hung up the phone with a sinking feeling — not because this new client had four boys, but because I knew none of us was free on Saturday.

"We've *got* to do something about this," I said. "We're in a jam. No one can take the job. Logan would be perfect for the Morgans. He's good with boys and he lives right nearby."

"But he doesn't want to join the club," said Kristy.

"I know. But couldn't we make him some kind of special member? Someone we could call when we need help, but who doesn't have to go to the meetings? That way everyone would be happy. Our club would look good because we'd be able to provide sitters instead of saying no one's available, Logan would get a job every now and then, and we wouldn't be embarrassed at the meetings."

"Well," said Kristy, "it really isn't a bad idea."

"Isn't a *bad* idea?! It's a great idea!" exclaimed Dawn. "Call him, Mary Anne."

"All right," I said. I waited for the usual nervousness to run through me, but I felt fine. I dialed Logan.

"Hello?" he answered.

"Guess who."

"I don't have to guess, I know," Logan replied. I could almost *hear* him smiling.

"Then guess where I am."

"At a Baby-sitters Club meeting."

"Very good! And guess what I'm going to ask you."

There was a pause. "To join the club?"

"No. I have a better idea. See, a whole bunch

137

of people have called today and, as usual, we're really busy. A new client just phoned — a man who lives across the street from the Rodowskys. He's got four boys, and none of us can sit. We don't want to turn him down the very first time he calls, so I thought of you. Do you want this job?"

"Yes, but . . . Mary Anne, I've got to tell you the truth. I don't want to come to your club meetings."

"Why not?" I asked, my heart thumping.

"Because they're too embarrassing. I didn't like being the only boy. And Claudia told that story about the . . . you know."

So Logan didn't want to say "bra strap" either.

"I know," I replied. I was glad that was the *only* reason he didn't like the meetings. "Well, to be honest, we were embarrassed, too. So that's why I was thinking you could be some special kind of club member — "

"An *associate* member," whispered Kristy.

"An associate member," I said. "And we'll only call on you when we really need extra help. You won't have to go to the meetings."

"Really?" said Logan. "Hey, great!"

"So you want to do it?"

"Definitely."

I put my hand over the mouthpiece. "He'll do it."

"I'll make it official," Kristy announced, gesturing for the phone. "Hi, Logan," she said. "I hereby make you an associate member of the Baby-sitters Club. . . . You do? Okay, sure. We'll need to meet them and stuff, but that's great."

Kristy handed the phone back to me, and I hung it up, wishing I could have said a more private good-bye to Logan.

"Guess what," said Kristy. "Logan knows a couple of other guys who might want to be associate members."

We all began talking. Then we called Mr. Morgan with the news that Logan Bruno would be baby-sitting.

I sat back and let the excitement sink in. Our club had *boy* members. Well, one anyway. I had Logan. The Fifties Fling was coming up. It was my thirteenth birthday. And when I went home after the meeting, Tigger would be there to greet me.

About the Author

ANN M. MARTIN did *a lot* of baby-sitting when she was growing up in Princeton, New Jersey. Now her favorite baby-sitting charge is her cat, Mouse, who lives with her in her Manhattan apartment.

Ann Martin's Apple Paperbacks are *Bummer Summer, Inside Out, Stage Fright, Me and Katie (the Pest)*, and all the other books in the Baby-sitters Club series.

She is a former editor of books for children, and was graduated from Smith College. She likes ice cream, the beach, and *I Love Lucy*; and she hates to cook.

Be sure to read all the books in the Baby-sitters Club series: